Robert F. Pennell

Rome

from the earliest times down to 476 A. D

Robert F. Pennell

Rome

from the earliest times down to 476 A. D

ISBN/EAN: 9783337382063

Printed in Europe, USA, Canada, Australia, Japan

Cover: Foto ©Andreas Hilbeck / pixelio.de

More available books at **www.hansebooks.com**

ROME,

FROM THE EARLIEST TIMES
DOWN TO 476 A.D.

COMPILED BY

R. F. PENNELL,

PROFESSOR OF LATIN IN PHILLIPS EXETER ACADEMY.

———∘o⦂ଡ଼⦂o∘———

BOSTON:
JOHN ALLYN, PUBLISHER.
1876.

PREFACE.

THIS book is intended to be a companion to my History of Greece. It is compiled chiefly from Mommsen and Niebuhr. For the entire history, from the Battle of Actium, and for portions previous to that date, I am indebted to Dr. D. F. WELLS, whose assistance I was obliged to ask on account of press of duties.

R. F. PENNELL.

THE PHILLIPS EXETER ACADEMY,
10 July, 1876.

GEOGRAPHY OF ITALY.

INTRODUCTION.

ITALY is a long, narrow peninsula in the southern part of Europe, situated between the 38th and 46th parallels of North Latitude. It is 720 miles long, from the Alps to the southern extremity of Bruttii; and 330 miles broad in its widest part, *i.e.* from the Little St. Bernard to the hills north of Trieste. Its area is about the same as that of the State of Nevada; viz., 110,000 square miles.

Italy is bounded on the north and north-west by the Alps; on the east by the Adriatic; on the south by the Mediterranean; and on the west by the Tyrrhenian sea. It may be divided, for convenience' sake, into **Northern, Central,** and **Southern** Italy.

Northern Italy included Liguria, Gallia Cisalpina, and Venetia. The chief towns of Liguria were Genua (Genoa), Nicæa (Nice), and Asta (Asti). The chief places of Venetia were Patavium and Aquileia. Gallia Cisalpina contained many flourishing cities. Among these, south of the Padus (Po), were Ariminum (Rimini), Bononia (Bologna), Mutina (Modena), Parma, Placentia, Ravenna; north of the Padus were Augusta Taurinorum (Turin), Cremona, Ticinum (Pavia), Mediolanum (Milan), Mantua, and Verona.

A

separated from Northern Italy by the rivers Rubicon and Mucra, included Etruria, Latium, and Campania on the west, Umbria, Picenum, and Samnium on the east. Of the many cities of Etruria, the following will be mentioned: Arretium, Caere, Cortona, Clusium, Faerii, Fæsulæ, Pisæ, Veii, and Volaterræ.

The most important city of Latium was Rome. In Campania were Capua, Cumæ, Herculaneum, Neapolis, Pompeii, and Salernum.

In Umbria were Iguvium, Sentinum, and Spoletium.

In Picenum, Ancona, and Asculum.

In Samnium, Beneventum.

SOUTHERN ITALY

included Lucania and Bruttii on the west; Apulia and Iapygia (or Messapia) on the east. The chief towns of Lucania were settled by the Greeks: they were Heracleia, Metapontum, Pandosia, Sybaris, and Thurii.

In Bruttii were Croton, Locri, and Rhegium.

Apulia, the most level of the countries south of the Rubicon, was a rich and fertile plain, well watered.

The chief places were Arpi, Canusium, Cannæ, and Venusia.

In Iapygia were Tarentum and Brundisium.

The mountains of Italy consist of two chains, the Alps and Apennines. The former separate Italy on the north and north-west from the rest of Europe, ranging from 4,000 to 15,000 feet in height, and with but few passes. The highest peak in this range is Mt. Blanc. The Apennines are merely a continuation of the Alps, and extend down through the whole length of Italy. The volcano of Vesuvius, so famous, is in Campania.

The plains of Italy are small, with but two exceptions : the plain of the Padus (Po), from 100 to 150 miles in width on either side of that river; and the plain in Apulia, mentioned above. There are small plains in Etruria, Latium, and Campania.

The rivers of Italy are very numerous. The largest river is the Padus, of about 400 miles in length, and draining most of Northern Italy.

Its chief tributaries on the north are the Ticinus and Mincius ; on the south, the Trebia.

Other rivers, emptying into the Adriatic, are the Athesis (Adige), Rubicon, Metaurus, Aternus, and Aufidus ; emptying into the Tyrrhenian sea are the Arnus, Tiber, Liris, and Volturnus.

There are many lakes in Italy ; but we shall mention only the Alban Lake, Lake Regillus, and Trasimenus.

The islands about Italy are very important.

Sicily (about 10,000 square miles, might be compared with New Hampshire in size) is triangular in shape, and for this reason called often by the poets Trinacria (with three promontories). It contains many important cities, as Syracuse, Agrigentum, Messana, Catana, Camarina, Gela, Selinus, Egesta (or Segesta), and Panormus.

Sicily is mountainous. The highest mountain is the volcano Ætna (10,700 feet).

Sardinia is of about the same size as Sicily. Corsica, directly north, is considerably smaller. Between Corsica and the mainland of Italy is the small island of Ilva (Elba) ; Igilium, off Etruria ; Capreæ, in the Bay of Naples ; Strongyle (Stromboli) and Lipara, north of Sicily ; also the Ægates Insulæ west of it.

IAPYGIANS AND ETRUSCANS.

CHAPTER I.

The Early Inhabitants of Italy.

So far as we know, the primitive inhabitants of Italy were divided into **three** races; viz., the **Iapygian, Etruscan,** and **Italian.**

The **Iapygians** were the first to people Italy. They came probably from the north over the Apennines, and were pushed south by later immigrations.

The colonies planted in early times by the Greeks on the southern coast of Italy possessed a superior civilization to that of the Iapygians, and was productive of a gradual improvement among them, until, finally, we lose sight of the old inhabitants as a distinct race, their language and customs becoming absorbed by their more polished colonists.

The **Etruscans**, at the time when Roman history begins, were a powerful and warlike race, far superior to the Latins in civilization and the arts of life. The origin of this people is a matter of controversy, and will probably never be known. Their dominion, at the period of highest prosperity, extended from the Alps as far south as **Lucania**, concentrating its strength chiefly in **twelve** cities, between the rivers **Arno** and **Tiber.**

In this region most of the monuments of Etruscan art have been found.

At an early period (according to Roman traditions, in the sixth century B.C.) the Etruscans were expelled from the valley of the Po by the less civilized Gauls, — a race of the Celtic stock, from whom, in Roman times, the valley of the Po derived the name of Gallia Cisalpina.

The Italians were of the same common ancestry as the Hellenes, their forefathers having come from one Aryan race, who lived, long before recorded history, somewhere in the western part of Central Asia.

While the Hellenes were settling in Greece, the Italians pushed further west, and passed over the Apennines into Italy.

At this time, the Italians had made considerable advance in civilization. They understood, to some degree, the art of agriculture; the building of houses; the use of wagons and of boats; of fire in preparing food, and salt for seasoning it. They could make out of copper and silver various weapons and ornaments; also, the husband and wife were recognized, and the dividing of people into clans (tribes).

That branch of the Italians known as the Latins inhabited a plain which is bounded on the east and south by mountains; on the west by the Tyrrhenian sea; on the north by the high lands of Etruria.

This plain, called Latium, — comprising a district of only 700 square miles (one-half as large as the State of Rhode Island), with a coast of only fifty miles, with no good harbors, — is watered by two rivers, the Tiber, and its tributary, the Anio. Hills emerge here and there; as Soracte in the north-east, and the promontory of **Circeium** in the south-west; **Janiculum**, near Rome; and the **Alban** range further south.

The **climate** is made unhealthy during the summer months by the malaria, which prevails to a great extent.

The **soil** is fairly productive.

The neighborhood of the Alban mountains is the healthiest part of Latium, and best adapted for a strong-hold; and so it was here, naturally, that the Latins built their first town, **Alba**.

Afterwards, many other towns sprung up, as **Lanuvium, Aricia, Tusculum, Tibur, Præneste, Roma, Laurentum, Lavinium**, &c.

All these towns were at first politically independent of one another, *i.e.* each was governed by a prince of its own, and a select body of elders and warriors who acted as advisers to the prince.

The inhabitants of these towns or communities (30 at first), owing to their common origin and interests, soon formed a perpetual league, and chose **Alba**, as the oldest town, to be the head of the league, and the place for all the people of Latium to assemble annually, and offer sacrifice to their common god, Jupiter (Latiaris).

Thus the **Latins** preserved their **individual** independence, and at the same time, by having this common centre for meeting at stated periods, and celebrating their festivals, laid the foundation of that national union which, in after ages, became so powerful.

CHAPTER II.

The Romans and their Early Government.

WE have learned the probable origin of the **Latins**; how they settled in Latium, and founded numerous towns. We have also taken a cursory glance at their manner of government. We shall now examine more particularly that one of the **Latin** towns which was destined soon to outstrip all her sisters in prosperity and power.

Fourteen miles from the mouth of the Tiber, the monotonous level of the plain through which the river flows is broken by a cluster of hills rising to a considerable height, around one of which once settled a tribe of **Latins** called **Ramnes** (gradually changed to **Romans**).

We have no means of ascertaining when this settlement was formed; tradition says in 753 B.C. In all probability it was centuries earlier.

The district included in the township of Rome at this time did not exceed 115 square miles.

The people were divided into **thirty** districts (curiæ), and each district into **ten** clans (gentes).

The chief ruler was a king, holding office for life, whose duties were **to command the army, to perform certain sacrifices, and to preside in the Senate.**

This body was a council of elders, who advised the king, and at his death directed the government until his successor was elected from their own body.

The original inhabitants assembled by districts (curiæ) from time to time, and were called the **Comitia Curiata**. This assembly alone had the power to change the laws, declare war or peace, and confirm the election of kings made by the Senate.

The original founders of Rome and their direct descendants were called the **Patricians**, who formed a class distinct from all others, jealously protecting their rights against all intruders.

Attached to the Patricians was a class of people called **Clients**, who, though personally free, had no civil rights (*i.e.* could take no part in the government), and were obliged to assist the Patrician to whom they were bound, in every way. In return, the Patricians gave them their support, and looked after all their interests.

There were also the **Slaves**, who were the mere property of their masters, and could be bought or sold at pleasure.

By the side of these **three** classes (viz. **Patricians, Clients, Slaves**), there gradually grew up another class, composed of the former inhabitants of conquered states and others who had fled to Rome for refuge.

This class, called **Plebeians** (multitude), the very name of which shows their numbers, belonged to no "**district**" or "**clan**," but were personally free, and allowed to own property and engage in trade.

The **Plebeians** were constantly increasing, and, as numbers give power, began to demand more rights. This demand was met by the so-called **Servian** reform of the constitution, the addition of a new assembly called the **Comitia Centuriata**, into which the Plebeians were admitted as citizens, and the whole population ranked according to property.

At the same time, all were called upon to serve in the armies, which service had been before performed by the **Patricians**.

The whole population was now divided into six classes, according to their property. The several classes were subdivided into 193 "centuries," each "century" representing the same amount of property.

The people thus classified met from time to time on the **Campus Martius**, a plain outside of the city, and voted upon subjects coming under their jurisdiction.

In this assembly, called, as stated above, the "**Comitia Centuriata**," each "century" had one vote, and its vote was decided by the majority of the individual voters.

The tendency of this system was to give to the wealthy the whole power; for, since each "century" represented the same amount of property, the "centuries" in the upper or **richer** classes were much smaller than those in the lower or **poorer** classes, so that a majority of the **centuries** might represent a small minority of the **people**.

1*

CHAPTER III.

The Consuls and Tribunes.

In the previous chapter, we learned something about the early government of the Romans.

This form of government, called the **regal** form, lasted for two or three centuries; but the abuse of the regal power led to the abolition of a **monarchy**; and in the place of one king, who held his office for life, **two consuls** were elected **annually** from the **Patricians**, each of whom possessed supreme power, and acted as a salutary check upon the other; so that neither was likely to abuse his power.

In great emergencies, a person could be appointed by one of the consuls, to have authority over all others, called the **Dictator**, whose tenure of office never exceeded six months.

It was at this time (about 500 B.C.) that the **Comitia Centuriata**, explained in the previous chapter, came to be a very important assembly of the people, superseding in a measure the **Comitia Curiata**.

All appeals in criminal cases were brought before this assembly; in it magistrates were nominated, laws adopted or rejected.

We have seen how the system of voting in the **Comitia Centuriata** left the power practically in the hands of a few of the wealthy. Yet this assembly was a gain for the **Plebeians**, as property was its basis; for many

Plebeians were very rich, and could take precedence of Patricians of less property.

Moreover, the Senate, which heretofore had consisted solely of **Patricians**, now admitted into its ranks a number not belonging to the nobility, called **Conscripti**, who, however, were not on the same footing as the old members, not being allowed to take part in debates or to hold magistracies.

In the Senate thus constituted, the nomination of all magistrates made in the **Comitia Centuriata** was confirmed or rejected. Thus it had control of the election of the consuls (whose duties, we must remember, were those of **supreme** administrators, judges, and generals, though every Roman citizen had a right to appeal from their decision to the Comitia Centuriata, in cases involving life).

Two subordinate officers, chosen from the Patricians, were appointed by the consuls, called **Quæstores**, whose duties were to manage the finances under the direction of the Senate.

The result of all these changes was that, although the **Plebeians** were admitted to a voice in the government through the Comitia Centuriata, yet the **Patricians** became more exclusive than ever, having, as they did, the control of the elections of the **Consuls** and **Quæstors**, and since all the sacred priesthoods were filled from their ranks.

This government, resting, as far as the **Plebeians** were concerned, upon a property basis, led to the amassing of a large amount of landed property by single individuals, and the crushing of the smaller landowners. The rich land-owners also increased their wealth immensely by "**farming**" the public revenues;

i.e., the Roman State would let out to them, for a good round sum, the collecting of all import duties and other revenues. They, in turn, would manage by extortion to enrich themselves very rapidly, and thus acquire great power. Hence only the **wealthy Plebeians**, with the **Patricians**, had any voice at all in the government. The rights of all the rest were utterly disregarded.

These became more and more oppressed, and only wanted a good opportunity to rise and remonstrate against their hard lot. They were much better off, they thought, under the old regal government; then they could make a tolerable and even comfortable living; then they were allowed to enjoy the public pasture; and, whenever new lands were conquered, portions of them were always assigned by the state to the poor for occupation; taxes then were not oppressive, nor were they obliged to sell or mortgage all they had, and even give up their own persons into slavery, to satisfy the demands of their creditors. They did not then see hundreds of their companions thrown into prison, because unable to pay their debts.

It is not strange, therefore, that they became uneasy.

The opportunity for rebelling against this unjust and cruel oppression was soon offered. Rome was hard pressed by a neighboring state, and needed extra men to defend her honor. One of the consuls liberated all who were confined in prison for debt, and, through their aid, the danger was averted.

Upon the return of the army, the other consul insisted upon enforcing the law for debt, and confined again all who had been set free, although they had done such good service for their city.

The next year Rome was threatened with the same danger. Again the prisoners were called upon to defend their city; but, remembering the reward of the previous year, they refused at first, and only consented finally when the higher authority of the Dictator was exercised.

Again, the Romans were victorious; but the idea of a second time being thrown into chains was so unendurable to the soldiers, that, when they arrived near their city walls, they deserted the general, and, marching in martial order to a hill near by, occupied it, threatening to found a new city in this the most fertile part of Latium, unless their oppressors were willing to make some concessions.

The Patricians and richer Plebeians saw that a reconciliation must be brought about, or their own ruin would be the result. Thus the seceders carried the day, and returned to the city.

The name of "**Sacred Mount**" was given to this hill by the Plebeians.

The results of the secession were felt throughout all Roman history, and marked a truly sacred era in the history of the common people.

A law was now passed that the **Plebeians** should choose annually from their own body two officers, called "**Tribuni Plebis**," who should look after their interests, and have the power of **vetoing** any action taken by any magistrate in the city.

For many years the **Consuls** and **Tribunes** represented, in a measure, opposing interests. The former had a **positive** power; *i.e.*, the power of **commanding**: the latter only a **negative** power; *i.e.*, that of **forbidding**. The latter had a more unlimited sway; for the

Consul was obliged to submit to any veto from him, while the **Tribune** never submitted to the **Consul** at all within the city. But, outside of the city walls, the **Tribunes** had no authority; and when the consuls assumed command (imperium) of the armies, their actions could be restrained in no way; also the **Dictator**, whose authority was of a military character, and exercised outside of the city, could not be interfered with by the **Tribunes**.

Two subordinate officers, chosen annually from the Plebeians, called **Ædíles**, held nearly the same position in reference to the **Tribunes** as the **Quæstors** to the **Consuls**.

They had special charge of the temple of Ceres, and derived their name from ædes (*temple*). In this temple were deposited for safe keeping all the decrees of the Senate.

The **Ædiles** also assisted the **Tribunes** in the performance of their various duties.

These two offices, the result of the secession, were filled every year by elections at first held in the **Comitia Centuriata**, but afterwards in an assembly called the **Comitia Tributa**, which met now inside and now outside of the city walls.

This assembly was composed chiefly of **Plebeians**, who voted by **tribes** (hence the name tributa = composed of tribes), each tribe being entitled to one vote, and its vote being decided by the majority of its individual voters.

Measures passed in this assembly were, at first, not binding upon the people at large; but, as we shall see, became soon as important as those passed in either the **Comitia Centuriata** or **Curiata**.

CHAPTER IV.

The Decemvirate. — Second Secession. —Valerio-
Horatian Laws, Licinian Rogations, Horten-
sian Law.

The aim of the Patricians was now to lessen the
power of the **Tribunes** in every way possible; that of
the Plebeians, to restrain the power of the **Consuls**, and
extend that of the **Tribunes**. Party spirit ran high;
even hand-to-hand contests took place in the streets
of Rome. Many families left the city, and settled in
neighboring places to escape the quarrels. It is a
wonder that the government held together at all, so
fierce were the passions on both sides.

The **Agrarian** laws are now first heard of. These
laws, which had reference to the distribution of the
public lands among the poorer classes, were violently
opposed by the **Patricians**. The first law, although
passed, cost its advocate (Spurius Cassius) his life, and
was itself never enforced.

These quarrels finally culminated in the murder of
one of the Tribunes (Gnæus Genucius) for attempting
to veto some of the proceedings of the consuls. A law
was now passed (471 B.C.) by the violent effort of the
Plebeians (called the Publilian Law, from Publilius,
its proposer), which enacted that the Tribunes should
be chosen in the **Comitia Tributa**, instead of the **Comi-**

tia Centuriata. Thus the Plebeians could now elect their Tribunes freely, and gained a step in power which they never lost.

For the next twenty years, the struggle between the rich and poor at Rome continued unabated. The demand of the latter was a written code of laws. Finally, it was arranged that the Comitia Centuriata should choose from the people at large ten men, called the Decemvirate, who should hold office for one year. These magistrates were to supersede all others, and direct the government. But their chief duty was to draw up a code of laws, and submit it to the approval of the people.

These laws were approved, and engraved on ten tables of copper, and were placed in the Forum in front of the Senate house. Two more tables were added the next year; making, in all, twelve, — the only Roman code.

The Decemviri should have resigned as soon as these laws were drawn up and approved; but they neglected to do so, and began gradually to act in a cruel and tyrannical manner.

The people grew more and more uneasy, and meditated a revolution, which broke out finally, when one of the Decemviri passed so unjust a sentence as to bring an innocent maiden into his own power for the gratification of his lusts. The father saved his daughter's honor by stabbing her to the heart; and, fleeing himself to the camp, he called upon the soldiers to put down so unjust a government.

A second time the army left their leaders, and seceded to the Sacred Mount, where they nominated their own tribunes. Then, marching into the city, they compelled the Decemviri to resign.

A compromise was now made with the Patricians, resulting in the Valerio-Horatian laws, the substance of which was as follows : —

I. Every Roman citizen could appeal to the Comitia Centuriata against the decision of the supreme magistrate.

II. All the decisions of the **Comitia Tributa** (called Plebiscita) were made binding (if sanctioned by the Senate and **Comitia Curiata**) upon the Patricians and Plebeians alike. This assembly now became of equal importance with the other two.

III. The person of the **Tribunes, Ædiles**, and other Plebeian officers, was to be considered sacred.

IV. The Tribunes could take part in the debates of the Senate, and veto any of its decisions.

Thus we see the Plebeians gradually gaining ground, notwithstanding the strenuous efforts of the Patricians to keep them down.

A few years after the Valerio-Horatian laws, the **Canuleian** law (445 B.C.) was passed, making valid any marriage between a Patrician and a Plebeian, and enacting that all children of such marriage should follow the rank of the father.

At the same time, in the place of the **two** consuls, **six military Tribunes** were elected annually by the Comitia Centuriata, the office being open to **all** citizens.

To offset this gain for the Plebeians, the Patricians obtained (435 B.C.) the appointment of two new officers, called **Censores**, elected from their own ranks in the **Comitia Centuriata** once in every **five** years, to hold office for **eighteen** months.

The duties of the **Censors** were : —

I. To see that the citizens of every class and order were properly registered.

II. To punish immorality by removal from the Senate of any of its members.

III. To have a general supervision of the finances and public works of the state.

This office became, in after years, the most coveted in Rome.

But again (421 B.C.) the Plebeians were amply compensated for this gain of the Patricians, by obtaining the right of electing one of their number as **Quæstor.** There were now **four Quæstors.**

Thus the nobility, in spite of the most obstinate resistance, sustained loss after loss. Even the **rich** Plebeians, who had heretofore generally found it for their interest to side with the Patricians, now joined the farmers and lower classes.

Finally (367 B. c.), the Tribunes of the Plebeians (Licinius and Sextus) proposed the following bills, called the **Licinian Rogations :** —

I. To abolish the six **military Tribunes,** who had superseded the two consuls, and reinstate the latter, **choosing one of them from the Plebeians.**

II. To forbid any citizen holding more than 500 jugera (300 acres) of the public lands, and feeding thereon more than 100 oxen and 500 sheep.

III. To compel all landlords to employ on their fields a certain number of **free** laborers, proportionate to the number of their slaves.

IV. To allow all interest hitherto paid on borrowed money to be deducted from the principal, and the rest be paid in three yearly instalments.   .

These Rogations, we see, were a great gain for the

poorer classes. It gave them an opportunity for labor, which had been done in so great a measure before by the slaves. They could feel less burdened by their debts, having some prospect of paying them.

But especially, since they had accession to the highest office at Rome, viz. the consulship, they felt that their interests would be better protected.

However, the struggle went on, with scarcely unabated energy, for nearly thirty years. The Plebeians had gained so much that they could not stop until they were placed on an equal footing with the nobility in civil rights.

First, they obtained the right of having the office of **Dictator** open to them ; then those of **Censor** and **Prætor**; until, finally, by the law of **Hortensius**, the Dictator (286 B.c), **all the decrees** (Plebiscita) of the **Comitia Tributa** stood on the same footing of equality with those of the **Comitia Centuriata**, not being conditional, as heretofore, upon the approval of the **Senate** and **Comitia Curiata**.

Thus the strife that had lasted for 200 years was virtually ended ; and although the Roman nobility still held aloof from the commons, yet their rights as citizens were no greater than those of the Plebeians.

CHAPTER V.

THE first authentic history of Rome begins about 400 B.C. The city then possessed but little beyond her own walls. She was surrounded by hostile peoples, ready to destroy her if an opportunity offered.

About this time, a barbarous tribe from Gaul (France) invaded Italy, and captured and sacked Rome. All records of the city's history were destroyed; and thus, previous to this date (390 B.C.), we have no reliable data.

It was nearly half a century before Rome recovered from the effects of the Gallic invasion, obliged, as she was, to struggle continually with neighboring states.

At this date (340 B.C.), Rome began a series of wars for the subjugation of Italy. Her strongest enemies were the **Samnites,** — a race who had established themselves in the mountainous districts of Central Italy, and early extended their authority over the entire Campania.

Between the Samnites and Romans a treaty had been made (354 B.C.). Since then, both had, independently of each other, been waging war against the Volsci. The Samnites went so far as to attack **Teanum**, a city of Northern Campania, which appealed to Capua for aid. The Samnites at once appeared before Capua, which, unable to defend itself, asked aid of Rome.

Alarmed at the advances of the Samnites, Rome only awaited an excuse to break her treaty. This was furnished by the Capuans surrendering their city unconditionally to Rome, so that, in attacking the Samnites, she would only be defending her subjects.

Thus began the

SAMNITE WAR,

which lasted for fifty years, with varying success, and was interrupted by two truces. Hence it is usual to divide it into three portions, and to describe them as the **First, Second,** and **Third** Samnite wars. It was fought with great stubborness on both sides, and the enemies were pretty evenly matched. The First Samnite war was speedily brought to a close, without any material advantage to either side, by a renewal of the class struggle at Rome, and also because the Latin allies were showing unequivocal symptoms of discontent. The civil strife resulted in the extension of the Licinian law of debt, so that debts were abolished altogether, and in the making of both consulships open to the common people. The Latins were only quieted by being subdued.

Hitherto the Latins had been allies to the Romans; but it now became necessary either to subdue them or to admit them to an equal share in the government, and form a single consolidated union. A proposition was sent to Rome by the Latins, by the terms of which they sue to have one of the two consuls and 300 members of the Senate; but it was rejected. The great Latin War (340–338 B.C.) followed, in the first year of which a battle was fought near **Vesuvius.** The Romans, with their Samnite allies, were victorious through

the efforts of the consul, **T. Manlius Torquatus**, one of
the illustrious names of this still doubtful period.
The remainder of the operations was rather a series
of expeditions against individual cities than a general
war.

By the Latin Conquest, not only Latium, but also the
country of the Volscians and Aruncans, was added to
Roman territory, and partitioned among the people.

It was the policy of Rome always to punish a fallen
enemy severely, but at the same time to hold out
to them, as inducement to future loyalty, a prospect
that they might by good conduct earn the privileges
of the most favored. At the same time, full or partial
citizenship was often granted to a portion of a conquered people, which influenced the remainder to strive
to attain a like position. In accordance with this
policy, some of the Latin communities were at once
incorporated with the Roman territory, while the rest
held the position of conquered country.

During the interval between the Latin and the
Second, or Great, Samnite wars, Rome occupied herself in strengthening her frontier, by placing colonies
along her Samnite boundary, and preparing for the
struggle which was inevitable. While thus engaged,
she constantly gave evidence of her determination to
renew the war. Privernum, one of the newly conquered Volscian cities, revolted (330 B.C.), but was soon
reduced. The deputies, being asked what was due to
such rebellious conduct, asked, " What is due to brave
men who have fought for freedom?" " Well, but if
we spare you?" " Peace, if you treat us well; if ill, a
speedy return of war," was the reply. The inhabitants
of Privernum were admitted to Roman citizenship.

Three years later (327 B.C.), the Senate sent to Palæopolis, a Greek town near Neapolis (Naples), to complain of outrages committed upon Roman subjects in Campania. Satisfaction was refused at the instigation of the Tarentines, a Greek colony of Southern Italy, whose representations were the more readily listened to, as, in case of war, the Samnites might be counted on for assistance against the common enemy, Rome. Palæopolis was utterly destroyed; and then the Senate turned their attention once more to the Samnites.

It was charged that, in addition to their **assistance** to **Palæopolis, they had instigated the revolt of Privernum.** The charges were indignantly denied, and war was declared. It will be observed that, whenever Rome found a powerful enemy, whom she was unable at once to crush, peace was made, which was but a truce for the purpose of strengthening positions and completing preparations for a renewal of war. These preparations were in themselves virtual, and often actual, demonstrations of hostility. In distress Rome was always ready for such a peace; but, when her position was more favorable, pretexts were never wanting on which to break it. Roman faith was kept with strangers only so long as it pleased Rome.

During the first five years (326–322 B.C.) of the war, the Romans were usually successful; and the Samnites were compelled to sue for peace. A truce of a year was granted, and then hostilities were renewed. By this time the Samnites had found a worthy leader in C. Pontius, by whose skill and wisdom the fortune of war was turned against the Romans during seven long years (321–315 B.C.). In the first year of his command, he induced the consuls to hasten to the assistance of the town of Luceria. Their way led them into a small plain, at each end of which was a defile. On gaining this plain, they found Pontius strongly posted to oppose them. After a bloody but fruitless attempt to force his position, a retreat was ordered; but, in the mean time, the defile in rear had been occupied, and nothing remained but a capitulation.

A treaty was signed by the consuls and all the superior officers, according to which peace was to be made, and every thing which had been taken from the Samnites was to be restored. Such was the affair at the Caudine Forks, — one of the most humiliating disgraces which ever befell the Roman arms. The army was made to pass under the yoke, stripped of every thing but their under-garments, and then suffered to depart. Rome was filled with dismay at the news. The citizens dressed in mourning; business and amusements were suspended; and every energy was devoted to repairing the disaster. The results of the deliberations were eminently characteristic of the people. Compliance was refused with the terms of the treaty, on the ground that the consuls had no authority to make a treaty; and it was determined to deliver the signers as prisoners to the enemy. This was done; but Pontius demanded either good faith, or the returning of the army to its position at the Forks.

War was renewed, and dragged on for seven years, when the Samnites were so utterly defeated by Fabius, who had been appointed Dictator, that they were unable to meet the Romans again on the field with any chance of success. The war was finally ended by the Samnites agreeing to relinquish all their sea-coast, giving up all alliances and conquests, and acknowledging the supremacy of Rome (304 B.C.).

The Samnites had only yielded to the direst necessity in concluding peace, and immediately set to work uniting Italy against Rome. In this they were so successful, that, after six years, began what is known as the Third Samnite war, under the leadership of **Gellius Egnatius**. The fortune of this war was determined in a sanguinary battle at **Sentium**, where the Samnites were entirely routed by Fabius and Decius, after a long and doubtful struggle, in which both Decius and Gellius lost their lives. The battles which followed during the five remaining years of the war only confirmed the supremacy of Rome.

With the exception of a fruitless rising, when the arrival of Pyrrhus seemed to offer an opportunity to retrieve their losses, the Samnites gave Rome no further trouble. The hero of the last two Samnite wars was **Q. Fabius**, by whose assistance his son won the final battle of the contest (290 B.C.). Pontius, who was once more in command of his countrymen, was taken prisoner, and, after gracing the triumph of father and son, was put to death in prison.

During the Samnite war, the gradual union of the Patricians and Plebeians continued. The Plebeians grew wealthy, those more destitute being sent off to colonize the new conquests; while the Patricians became more used to the division of honors. But a new class had forced itself into notice, — the **Freedmen**. Under this name are included those who were descended from slaves, as well as those who had been liberated from bondage. They were, many of them, wealthy, and their numbers had increased, so that they

2

would have become a power, had not their citizenship been limited by restricting them to one of the four city tribes. They were placed by Appius Claudius on the lists of any tribe they might select. Thus they would have made themselves a third element, constantly increasing in influence, had they not, five years later, been restored by Q. Fabius and P. Decius (307 B.C.) to their four city tribes; so that, no matter how powerful they became, their voice might be readily neutralized by the action of the remaining tribes.

CHAPTER VI.

PYRRHUS (281–272 B.C.).

In the early times of Rome, while, indeed, she was scarcely known even to her own neighbors, it had been the custom of the Greeks to send their colonies away from home to relieve the pressure of too rapid increase. We find them in Spain, France, Asia Minor, and notably in the island of Sicily and South Italy, where the country became so thoroughly Grecianized that it received the name of Græcia Magna.

Here were many fine and flourishing cities, such as Syracuse, Tarentum, Sybaris, Croton, and Thurii. These had, by the time of their contact with Rome, greatly fallen from their former grandeur, partly from the inroads of barbarians from the north, partly from civil dissensions, and still more from their jealousies of one another; so that they were unable to oppose any firm and united resistance to the southern progress of the Roman arms. It had been their custom to rely largely upon strangers for the recruiting and management of their armies, — a fact which explains the ease with which they were overcome.

Of these cities, Tarentum was now the chief; and with it a treaty had been made by which the Tarentines agreed to certain limits beyond which their fleets were not to pass, the Romans binding themselves not to allow their vessels to appear in the Gulf of Tarentum, nor their armies to pass a particular temple

(Lacinian Juno). As usual, the Romans found no difficulty in evading this treaty whenever it should profit them.

Thurii was attacked by Lucanians, and, despairing of aid from Tarentum, called on Rome for protection. As soon as domestic affairs permitted, war was declared against the Lucanians, and the wedge was entered which was to deliver Grecian Italy to Rome. Pretending that the war was instigated by the Tarentines, the Romans decided to ignore the treaty, and sent a little fleet of ten vessels into the Bay of Tarentum. It was a gala day, and the people were assembled in the theatre overlooking the bay when the ships appeared. It was determined to punish them. A fleet was manned, and four of the Roman squadron were destroyed.

A demand for satisfaction was treated with insult and contempt; so the next year one of the consuls was ordered to the south. The Tarentines had already sent envoys, asking aid from **Pyrrhus**, the young and ambitious king of Epeirus, who hoped, by a powerful western empire, to overmatch the exhausted monarchies of the east, which had risen on the death of Alexander of Macedon (281 B.C.).

Pyrrhus landed in Italy with a force of 20,000 foot, about 3,000 horse, and 20 elephants, and at once set about compelling the effeminate Greeks to prepare for their own defence. Places of amusement were closed; the people were forced to do military duty; disturbers of the public safety were put to death; and other reforms were made which the dangers of the situation seemed to demand.

The armies met on the plain of **Heracleia** (280 B.C.),

where the level nature of the country was every way in favor of the Grecian method of fighting. The Romans were defeated : their horses would not face the elephants ; but, in spite of all, they retired in good order. Pyrrhus is said to have been much impressed by the heroic conduct of the foe, and to have remarked : " Another such victory will send me back without a man to Epeirus." He recognized the inferior qualities of his allies, and determined to make a peace. A trusted messenger was sent to Rome ; but he received for answer to his propositions, that Rome would not treat of peace till Pyrrhus should leave Italy.

Pyrrhus then tried force, and, hastily advancing northward, soon appeared within eighteen miles of Rome, having carried every thing before him. Here his danger became great. The defection he had hoped among the Latins did not take place ; and the armies which had been operating elsewhere were now ready to unite against himself. He therefore retired to winter quarters at Tarentum ; and there received the famous embassy of C. Fabricius, sent to propose an interchange of prisoners. It was in vain that bribes and threats were employed to shake the courage of the men sent by the Senate ; and, on his part, Pyrrhus refused to grant the exchange desired.

Hostilities were renewed. The Romans were defeated at the plain of Apulian **Asculum** (279 B.C.) ; but it was only another of those Pyrrhic victories which are almost as disastrous as defeat. Pyrrhus soon after made peace with the Romans, and retired to Sicily to operate against the Carthaginians, where he remained above two years. The next time he met the Romans was near **Beneventum** (274 B.C.), where he was utterly routed. By this time the Romans had become used to the elephants, and used burning arrows against them. The wounded became furious and unmanageable, and threw the army into confusion. With the battle at Beneventum ended the career of Pyrrhus in Italy. He returned home, and, two years later, was accidentally killed by a woman at Argos.

The departure of Pyrrhus left all Italy at the mercy of Rome; but the conquest was yet to be completed. Tarentum was still in the hands of Milo, a general of Pyrrhus; the various nations who had espoused the cause of the Greeks were still in arms; and the north was still hostile. But among her enemies there was nowhere any head or unity; while Rome acted with both prudence and energy.

Rome showed as much prudence in her policy for the retaining her conquests, as she did bravery in their acquisition. She did this by separating them from each other with the utmost care, and by making them dependent on herself to the greatest possible extent. By making the interests of each distinct and individual, she prevented any union which might be dangerous; while, by her control of those interests, she prevented defection.

In accordance with this plan, her dependencies were divided into three classes. The **Prefectures** were ruled by an officer appointed at Rome; their condition resulted from their attempts to throw off the Roman yoke. The inhabitants were subjected to all the burdens of citizenship, with none of its privileges. The **Municipal Towns** ruled themselves, were exempt from all but local taxation, and held their position by treaty. They were obliged, however, to furnish a military contingent, and, except by special act, could not enjoy the political or public rights of citizenship. The Colonies consisted either of Roman soldiers and their families, who were placed in strong and fortified places for the purpose of overawing the inhabitants, or parties of citizens who took up their abode in the conquered districts. In either case, they formed a firm protection against revolt; and in the latter, a valuable relief for the poorer classes. There were also, at this time, certain towns independent of Roman rule, and only bound by treaties; these, however, gradually disappeared as Rome grew more powerful, and took their places among the municipal towns.

Even at this early date, the necessity of easy communication with the capital seems to have been well understood. Roads were pushed in every direction, — broad, level roads, over which intelligence might be speedily carried or armies marched; they were chains which bound her possessions indissolubly together. Some of them remain to-day, — a monument of Roman thoroughness, enterprise, and sagacity, and the wonder and admiration of modern road-builders. By these means did Rome fasten solidly together the constantly increasing fabric of her empire, so that not even the successes of Hannibal could cause more than a momentary shaking of fidelity, for which ample punishment was both speedy and certain.

CHAPTER VI.

FOREIGN CONQUEST. — CARTHAGE. — FIRST PUNIC
WAR (264–241 B.C.).

WHILE Rome was gradually enlarging her territory
from Latium to the Straits of Messana ; on the other
shore of the Mediterranean, opposite Italy, and less
than 100 miles from Sicily, sprung up, through industry
and commerce, the Carthaginian power.

Like Rome, Carthage had an obscure beginning ; as
in the case of Rome, it required four centuries to form
its power.

It was the policy of Carthage to make a successful
revolt of her subdued allies an impossibility, by con-
suming all their energies in the support of her immense
population and the equipment of her numerous fleets
and armies. Hence all the surrounding tribes, once
wandering nomads, were compelled to become tillers
of the soil ; and, with colonies sent out by herself,
they formed the so-called Libyo-Phœnician population,
open to the attack of all, and incapable of defence.

The country around Carthage was thus very weak ;
and, the moment a foreign enemy landed in Africa,
the war was merely a siege of its chief city.

The power of Carthage lay in her commerce.
Through her hands passed the gold and pearls of the
Orient ; the famous Tyrian purple ; ivory, slaves, and
incense of Arabia ; the silver of Spain ; the bronze of
Cyprus ; and the iron of Elba.

But the harsh and gloomy character of the people; their cruel religion, which sanctioned human sacrifice; their disregard for the rights of others; and their well-known treachery, — shut them off from the higher civilization of Rome and Greece.

The government of Carthage was an **aristocracy**. A council composed of a few of high birth, and another of the very wealthy, managed the state. Only in times of extraordinary danger were the *people* summoned and consulted.

Rome was now (280 B.C.) a great power. Italy, from the Rubicon south, was under her control. The city itself was strongly fortified, and most of its subject towns were walled; thus forming a chain, as it were, of fortresses commanding the whole of Italy.

In leaving Sicily, Pyrrhus cried out, " What a beautiful battle-field for Rome and Carthage! " Neither could afford to give up to any rival power this great island situated in the centre of the Mediterranean, almost touching Italy, and within sight of Africa.

If Carthage was mistress of it, Rome would be shut up in her own peninsular; if Rome was in possession of it, the commerce of Carthage was intercepted, and a good breeze of one night would bring the Roman legions to her walls.

Three powers shared the island, — Hiero, king of Syracuse; the Carthaginians; and the Mamertines, a band of robbers, coming from Campania.

The latter had made Messana their head-quarters, and from there devastated the whole island. Hiero had managed to drive them back into Messana, and there besieged them. They now applied to Rome for assistance. The ambition of Rome was a mixture of

2*   c

pride and avidity: she wished to command, because
she believed herself already the greatest power of the
world; she wished to make conquest, because she could
enrich her treasure; and Sicily was such a rich prey.
Therefore, although she was in alliance with Hiero, and
had but recently executed 300 mercenaries for doing
the same thing in Rhegium that the Mamertines had
done in Sicily, she determined to aid them. But,
while making preparations to send troops, the Carthaginians had, as a neutral power, arranged a peace between Hiero and the Mamertines; the siege of Messana
was raised; the Carthaginian fleet lay in the harbor;
and a Carthaginian garrison, commanded by Hanno,
held possession of the citadel.

The Mamertines, now under Carthaginian influence,
informed the Romans, with thanks, that they no longer
needed their aid.

Nevertheless, the Roman commander, Claudius,
pushed on to Messana, succeeded in landing, and compelled Hanno to give up the citadel.

Thus the Romans gained their first foothold outside
of Italy.

A double alliance was formed with Messana and
Syracuse; and the whole of the eastern coast of Sicily
was under Roman control.

Two legions were sent to the island the next year
(262 B.C.), who, aided by the Sicilian Greeks, compelled
the Carthaginians everywhere to take refuge in their
fortresses.

Hannibal, son of Gisco, commander-in-chief of the
Carthaginians, collected the best of his troops into
Agrigentum, their most important inland city. The
Romans besieged the city for some time, until the gar-

rison, numbering 50,000, began to suffer from want of food. At this point, Hanno, the Carthaginian admiral, landed at Heracleia, and cut off the supplies of the Romans.

Both the besieged and besiegers at Agrigentum now suffered much. A battle was decided upon to bring the matter to an issue. In this battle, the Roman cavalry proved as inferior to the Carthaginian cavalry as did the Carthaginian infantry to the Roman infantry; but the infantry decided the day, and Agrigentum fell into the hands of the Romans. The whole of Sicily was now in their power, except a few maritime fortresses held by Hamilcar, the successor of Hanno.

The Romans now began to feel the need of a fleet. That of the Carthaginians ruled the sea without a rival: it not only kept control of many of the seaports of Sicily, but also threatened Italy itself.

The energy evinced by the Romans in building a fleet is very remarkable. A wrecked Carthaginian vessel was taken as a model; and, by the spring of 260 B.C., a fleet of 120 sail was ready for use.

The ships were made the more formidable by a heavy iron beak, for the purpose of running down and sinking the enemy's vessels; also a kind of hanging stage was placed on the front of the ship, which could be lowered in front or on either side. It was furnished on both sides with parapets, and had space for two men in front. On coming to close quarters with the enemy, this stage was quickly lowered, and fastened to the opposing ship by means of grappling-irons; thus enabling the Roman marines to board with ease their opponent's ship, and carry on the fight as if on land.

In 260 B.C., the Roman consul and admiral, Gnæus
Cornelius Scipio, set sail for Messana with the vanguard
of the fleet, consisting of 17 sail. On his way, he attempted to surprise Lipara, but was captured, with all
his vessels, by a division of the Carthaginian fleet stationed at Panormus.

The main part of the Roman fleet, however, sailed
soon after for Messana. It was commanded by the
second consul, **Gaius Duilius.**

The Carthaginians, commanded by Hannibal, son of
Gisco, sailed from Panormus, and met the Roman fleet
off the promontory of **Mylæ**, to the north-west of
Messana.

In this, the first naval contest of any importance between the Romans and Carthaginians, the comparative
merit of their fleets was tested. The newly invented
" stages," or boarding-bridges, of the Romans, were
found to be very efficient. The enemy could not approach near without these bridges descending with
their grappling-irons, and joining them fast to the Roman vessel.

The Romans were victorious; and nearly half of the
enemy's fleet was either sunk or captured.

The effect of the victory off Mylæ was very great.
Rome suddenly became a naval power. She could
now protect her commerce, and wrest from Carthage
the sole control of the seas.

A bronze column, composed of the beaks of the captured vessels, was erected in Rome in honor of this
victory of Duilius. The pedestal of it is still standing,
on which are inscribed some of the oldest inscriptions
in the Latin tongue.

Two plans were now open to the Romans; viz.,

either to attack the strongholds of the Carthaginians, on the coasts of Sicily, Sardinia, and Corsica, or to carry the war into Africa, and harass the Carthaginians in their own homes.

The former plan was first adopted. The year after the battle of Mylæ (259 B.C.), the consul, Lucius Scipio, captured Aleria, a seaport of Corsica; thus making the island a naval station against Sardinia.

No other permanent progress, however, was made by the Romans for some time. In 257 B.C., an unde-cisive, though hard-fought, naval engagement took place off the promontory of **Tyndaris**.

In 256 B.C., the Romans, becoming weary of their want of progress, decided to carry the war into Africa. Accordingly, a fleet of 330 sail, containing 100,000 sailors and a land army of 40,000, was ordered to at-tack Africa. The two consuls, **Marcus Atilius Regulus** and **Lucius Manlius Volso**, were in command.

The Carthaginian fleet, composed of 350 sail, and manned by as many troops as the Roman fleet, met it off **Ecnomus**.

After a bloody battle, in which 30 Carthaginian and 24 Roman vessels were sunk, and 64 of the enemy's ships captured, the Punic fleet hastened to the coast of Africa, and prepared, in the Gulf of Carthage, for a second battle. But the Romans sailed to the eastern side of the peninsular, which helps to form the Gulf of Carthage, and landed without opposition.

After fortifying a camp on a hill near **Clupea**, the Romans pillaged the surrounding country, and sent as many as 20,000 slaves to Rome. .

The Carthaginians were disheartened; the towns in the vicinity of Carthage surrendered, and the capital itself was in danger. They sued for peace; but the conditions proposed were too humiliating to be accepted. Seeing that they must fight, they occupied the winter in active preparations. With their gold they were enabled to hire large forces, among them the celebrated Spartan captain, **Xanthippus,** whose talent as a commander was great.

In the mean while, the Roman general, **Regulus,** remained inactive at **Tunes,** near Carthage, neglecting even to secure a line of retreat to his fortified camp at **Clupea.**

In the following spring (255 B.C.), the Carthaginians were ready for the field, and determined to attack Regulus before he could receive re-enforcements from Rome.

Regulus foolishly accepted battle, although greatly outnumbered in cavalry by his opponents. His own cavalry, stationed upon the wings (as was the custom in Roman armies), was immediately put to flight by the Carthaginian horsemen, and his infantry outflanked.

Although the Romans fought bravely, it was of no avail; they were cut down, but few escaping to Clupea. Regulus himself was captured, and died afterwards in Carthage.

The Romans, as soon as they heard of this defeat, sent a fleet of 350 sail to the aid of their forces shut up in Clupea. On its way, it gained a victory over the Carthaginians off the **Hermean** promontory, sinking 114 of their ships. The fleet arrived off Clupea just in time to save its friends. The Romans, very foolishly, evacuated their position, and, abandoning their numerous African allies, set sail for Italy.

Had the Romans sent re-enforcements to Regulus, they would have prevented this humiliating defeat, and probably ended the war with Carthage for ever, by destroying the city.

On its return home, the Roman fleet was overtaken by a severe storm, in which three-fourths of the vessels were wrecked, and their crews drowned; only eighty reached port.

The Romans were obliged now to build a new fleet; and in the course of three months 220 new vessels were ready for use.

In the spring of 254 B.C., this fleet, with the remnants of the old one, — numbering in all about 300 vessels, — appeared on the northern coast of Sicily, and captured **Panormus**, the most important seaport of the Carthaginians. Soon after, some smaller places fell into the hands of the Romans, until, of the north coast of the island, **Thermæ** alone remained under the Punic control.

In the following year (253 B.C.), the consuls, instead of following up their advantage in Sicily, preferred to try another attack upon Africa, and to plunder the coast towns. They accomplished their object, but, upon their return, were overtaken by another storm, and lost 150 ships.

In the year 252 B.C., Thermæ and the island of Lipara were captured by the Romans. The next year (251 B.C.), the consul, **Gaius Cæcilius Metellus**, gained a brilliant land victory over the enemy, the result of which was that **Eryx** fell into the hands of the Romans (249 B.C.). **Drepana** and **Lilybæum** were the only places in Sicily now held by the Carthaginians.

A regular siege of Lilybæum was decided upon, and

accordingly the city was blockaded by land and sea; but the besieging party suffered fully as much as the besieged, as their supplies were frequently cut off by the cavalry of the Carthaginians, and their ranks began to be thinned by disease.

Disheartened at the want of success, a sudden attack was ordered to be made by the blockading squadron upon the Carthaginian fleet stationed at Drepana.

The attack was unsuccessful; and more than three-fourths of the Roman squadron was captured.

This was the only great naval victory gained by the Carthaginians during the war.

Also a fleet of 120 vessels, sent with provisions to aid the blockading squadron at Lilybæum, was wrecked by a severe storm.

The Romans were now in perplexity. The war had lasted for fifteen years. They had lost four large fleets and one-sixth of their fighting population.

They had tried a landing in Africa, but had failed. They had attempted to storm Sicily, place by place. The smaller places had fallen; but the two strongest, Lilybæum and Drepana, stood more invincible than ever. What were they to do? They became despondent and inactive, and almost entirely abandoned their fleet; while on land they allowed the war to languish and nearly die out.

Had the Carthaginians been energetic, now would have been the time to humble their antagonist. But, having got rid of the Roman fleet, they foolishly allowed their own also to fall into decay, and contented themselves with petty warfare in and around Sicily.

Thus for six years (248–243 B.C.) the war dragged along ingloriously for both parties.

During this period (247 B.C.), **Hamilcar Barca** (*i.e.* lightning) was placed in command of the Carthaginians in Sicily. A man of great activity and military genius, entertaining the most bitter hatred against the Romans, he found it hard to endure the apathy and apparent indifference of the government at home.

Yet, with so much to contend against, he slowly gained power over the Romans in the island. No Roman general was a match for him. His privateers were continually appearing upon the Italian coast, and plundering the neighboring towns.

In a word, he was in a fair way of accomplishing from Sicily with his fleet what his more famous son afterwards undertook from Spain with a land force.

Finally, some private Romans of wealth, fearing that the Senate would never arouse from its state of inactivity, built, at their own expense, a fleet of 200 ships, and manned it with 60,000 sailors.

This fleet, placed under command of the consul, **Gaius Lutatius Catulus**, occupied the harbors of Lilybæum and Drepana in 242 B.C. The Carthaginians were taken by surprise, and equipped a fleet in such haste that it was very inefficient; so that, the following spring (241 B.C.), when it met the Romans off the **Ægates Insulæ**, it was utterly defeated. The honor of this victory belonged to the prætor, **Publius Valerius Falto**, who had succeeded the wounded consul in command.

Hamilcar thus saw the fruits of his heroic labors of seven years undone by the **haste** of others.

Sicily was surrendered, and peace made. Carthage agreed to pay the costs of the war, — about $3,000,000; one-third down, the remainder in ten annual payments.

Thus ended the **First Punic War**, — one of the

longest the Romans ever waged, the final battles of which were fought by soldiers who were not born when the war began.

The war, as a whole, was marked by many blunders on the part of both Romans and Carthaginians. The former had not yet learned the character of their enemy, and that a war with Carthage meant something different from one with Samnium. The wretched system of the Romans, of changing commanders every year, shut off even an able general from perfecting his plans.

Again, had the Carthaginians seconded their ablest commander, Hamilcar Barca, in his endeavors to recover Sicily and gain a foothold in Italy, the result of this war would have undoubtedly been far different.

Thus Rome had to thank the gods and the errors of her opponents for her victory, far more than her own prowess or skill.

CHAPTER VII.

Rome and Carthage between the First and Second Punic Wars (241–218 b.c.).

Twenty-three years elapsed between the First and Second Punic Wars.

The Carthaginians were occupied the first few years in putting down a rebellion of their neighboring subjects.

Rome, taking advantage of the position in which Carthage was placed, took possession of Sardinia, and, when Carthage objected, threatened to renew war, and obliged her to pay a fine of over one million dollars (237 b.c.).

Shortly after, Rome also annexed Corsica.

The acquisition of the islands of Sicily, Sardinia, and Corsica introduced a new system in the government of Rome; viz., the **provincial** system.

Heretofore, the two chief magistrates of Rome, the consuls, had exercised their functions over all the Roman possessions.

Now Sicily was made what the Romans called a **provincia**, or province. (Sardinia and Corsica formed another province.) Over each province was appointed an officer, called **proconsul**, who was inferior in rank to the consul, and equal to the prætor; whose duties combined those of commander-in-chief, chief magistrate, and supreme judge.

The finances of the provinces were intrusted to one or more **quæstors.** The dependants of Rome in Italy were obliged to furnish a certain number of troops to her army and navy; but her **provincial** dependants, instead of this burden, paid a **tenth** of their produce, and five per cent of the value of their imports and exports, into the Roman treasury.

About this time, the commerce of the Adriatic sea suffered much from the depredations of the **Illyrian** pirates. Ambassadors were sent from Rome to remonstrate with the king of the Illyrians; and since not only no satisfactory answers were given, but also one of the ambassadors was murdered on his return home, by the order of the king of Illyricum, as it was said, Rome had no alternative but to declare war.

A fleet was sent up the Adriatic in 229 B.C.; and the sea was cleared of pirates. The Illyrians on the coast were made dependants of Rome; and the Greek cities of Epidamnus, Corcyra, and Apollonia, attached themselves to her.

Thus most of the stations in the Adriatic became subject, like Sicily and Sardinia, to the authority of Rome.

In 225 B.C., Rome began the subjugation of the country between the Rubicon and the Alps. This tract of land, watered by the Po, and by far the most fertile in Italy, was in the hands of barbarous Gallic tribes.

In a short time (three years), the whole of this country, called Cisalpine Gaul (*i.e.* Gaul this side of the Alps), was subdued.

Colonies were planted by Rome in various localities in this newly acquired territory, in order to maintain a stronger possession.

The most important of these were Placentia, Cremona, Mutina.

The **Flaminian** Way, already completed as far as Spoletium, was continued to Ariminum, thus giving a direct road from Rome to the valley of the Po.

While Rome was thus rapidly gaining power, Carthage was not idle. As soon as the revolt mentioned above (page 43) had been subdued (237 B.C.), through the efforts of Hamilcar Barca, a project was formed of obtaining Spain in compensation for the loss of Sicily, Sardinia, and Corsica. Between 236 and 228 B.C., Hamilcar established a firm foothold in the whole of Southern and South-eastern Spain.

At the death of Hamilcar, his son-in-law, Hasdrubal, carried on the conquest. Many towns also were built; trade prospered; agriculture flourished. Rich silver mines about **Carthago Nova** were discovered, and enriched the treasury at home.

Hamilcar was assassinated in 220 B.C. **Hannibal**, his eldest son, was now looked to by all. He was still a young man, in his twenty-ninth year; but his life had been one of varied experience. While yet a boy, he had followed his father to the camp, and soon distinguished himself. His light and firmly built frame made him an excellent runner and fencer, and a fearless rider. The privation of sleep did not affect him; and he knew, like a soldier, how to enjoy or to want his food.

He entered the army at an early age, and learned his first lessons in fighting under his father's eye, whom he saw fall by his side.

At the accession of Hasdrubal (his sister's husband), he commanded the cavalry, and distinguished himself by brilliant personal bravery, as well as by his talents as a leader.

Such was the person now called upon to lead the Carthaginians, and one worthy of the trust. He was a great man wherever he went, and riveted the eyes of all.

Hannibal resolved to commence war as soon as elected to the chief command. He laid siege (219 B.C.) to **Saguntum**, a town of Spain allied to Rome; and thus virtually declared war with Rome herself.

In eight months, Saguntum surrendered; and the Roman ambassadors appeared at Carthage, demanding satisfaction.

When they declared that they were ready for peace or war, the Carthaginians accepted the latter (in the spring of 218 B.C.)

Thus the **Second Punic** War was declared.

CHAPTER VIII.

The Second Punic War. — Hannibal's March from Spain to Italy.

Hannibal set out in the spring of 218 b.c. from New Carthage with his army. It consisted of 90,000 infantry, and 12,000 cavalry, and 37 elephants. With this force, he intended to invade Italy. The Romans had at their disposal more than 500,000 troops, and a fleet of 220 quinqueremes.

With this large force, they were still dilatory, and neglected their own interests.

When Hannibal had practically declared war by attacking Saguntum the year before, they should have sent an army immediately into Spain, and saved the town.

But after Saguntum finally surrendered, and the war had been formally declared, the Romans could have massed an army on the banks of the Ebro, and there met Hannibal. They neglected to do even this.

Finally, however, an army and fleet were made ready, not to meet Hannibal, but for an expedition into Africa; while only a small force was sent, under the consul, **Publius Cornelius Scipio,** to the Ebro. But he proceeded leisurely; and, when an insurrection broke out on the Po, he employed the army ready for embarkation in suppressing the revolt, and levied new legions for the Spanish expedition.

Thus Hannibal reached the Pyrenees without meeting any Roman army. He was violently opposed, however, by the Spanish allies of the Romans, and was occupied about two months in conquering them.

At the Pyrenees, Hannibal sent home a part of his troops, retaining 50,000 infantry and 9,000 cavalry, all veteran forces. With these, he crossed the mountains without difficulty; then he marched along the coast by **Narbo** (Narbonne) and Nemausus (Nîmes), through the Celtic territory, with but little opposition. He arrived at the Rhone, opposite **Avenio** (Avignon), the last of July. There he first met the Romans.

Meanwhile, the consul, Scipio, had voyaged leisurely towards Spain, touching at Massilia (Marseilles) towards the end of June. Learning there that he was too late to intercept Hannibal in Spain (for he had already crossed into Gaul), he resolved to meet the Carthaginians on the Rhone.

Massilia was friendly to the Romans; and through her influence the Celtic tribes of that region were induced to assist Scipio in his attempt to check Hannibal. When the latter arrived at the Rhone, only a body of **Celtic** troops were ready to oppose his crossing; while the main army of Scipio, consisting of 22,000 infantry and 2,000 cavalry, were still in Massilia, **four** days' march distant.

It was Hannibal's policy to cross the Rhone before Scipio arrived with his troops. He bought up all the boats that could be found in the region, and constructed numerous rafts, so as to enable him to transport his forces in a body.

He also sent a detachment up the river, with orders to cross at the first available place, and, returning on the other bank of the river, surprise the Celtic forces in the rear.

Hannibal's plan worked admirably. At a given signal, the attack was made upon the rear of the Celtic camp, and ·the crossing of the troops begun. The Celts were taken by surprise, and fled, offering but little resistance.

Hannibal now was sure of an unobstructed march to the Alps.

Scipio, while Hannibal was **acting**, was holding councils in Massilia as to the best method of obstructing the enemy's crossing. Although the Carthaginian was delayed **five** days before he could perfect his plans for crossing, yet Scipio neglected to send aid to the Celts; and, when finally he did move, Hannibal's rear was three days' march from Avenio.

Scipio returned to Massilia in disgust. His course now should have been to embark his troops for Northern Italy, and make preparations to meet Hannibal as soon as he crossed the Alps. But he seemed to go from one blunder to another. The main body of his forces was sent to Spain, under his brother, **Gnæus Scipio**; and he himself, with a few men, sailed for Pisæ.

Meanwhile, Hannibal hurried up the valley of the Rhone, across the Isara (Isere), through the fertile country of the Allobroges, arriving in **sixteen** days at the crossing of the first Alpine chain (over **Mont du Chat**). Crossing this pass with some difficulty, owing to the nature of the country and the resistance of the Celts, he hastened on through the country of the **Centrones**, along the north bank of the Isara. As he was leaving this river, and approaching the foot of the pass of the Little St. Bernard, he was again attacked by the Celts, and obliged to make the ascent amidst continual and bloody encounters. Finally, after toiling a day and night, the army reached the summit of the pass. Here, on a table-land (the source of the river Dora), Hannibal allowed his troops a brief rest.

The hardships of the descent were even greater than those of the ascent.

The fertile valley of the Po must have been a welcome sight to the half-famished and exhausted soldiers, when, in the middle of September, they encamped, and were suffered to recruit their worn-out energies.

This was the time for Scipio to have had his army ready to attack the Carthaginians.

Had the Romans met them before they had recovered from their hard march, Hannibal's chances for victory would have been slight.

This march of Hannibal from the Rhone, so famous, of over 500 miles, through hostile countries, over high mountains, lasted for thirty-three days, and cost him 20,000 infantry and 3,000 cavalry.

CHAPTER IX.

THE SECOND PUNIC WAR.—FROM THE PASSAGE OF
THE ALPS TO THE BATTLE OF CANNÆ.

WHEN Hannibal arrived in Italy, the Romans were
unprepared to meet him. One of their armies was in
Spain under Gnæus Scipio; the other in Sicily (under
the consul, Sempronius), on its way to Africa.

A recent insurrection of the Gauls, in the valley of the
Po, though put down (see page 47), had compelled the
Romans to leave some troops in that vicinity to over-
awe their rebellious subjects. These were the only
forces immediately available against Hannibal.

The consul, Publius Scipio, who had arrived from
Massilia, took command of these forces. They were
inferior in numbers and discipline to the Carthaginian
troops; and in the first encounter, a cavalry engagement, the Romans were discomfited. This skirmish
(October, 218 B.C.)—for it was hardly worthy of the
name of battle—was fought near the river Ticinus, a
tributary of the Po. The consul himself was wounded,
and his life saved by his son, a lad of seventeen, afterwards the famous Scipio Africanus. The loss of the
Romans was considerable.

The Romans now retreated rapidly, crossing the Po at
Placentia, and destroying the bridge behind them. Here
(at the confluence of the Trebia and Po) Sempronius,
the other consul, was face to face with the army of Hannibal, drawn up on a field chosen by himself. The bat-

tle (December, 218 B.C.) was lost, unless the main body crossed the stream : hungry, weary, and wet, the Romans came on, and hastened to form in order of battle ; the cavalry, as usual, on the wings, the infantry in the centre. In the engagement that followed, the Roman cavalry was quickly repulsed by the Carthaginian ; but the in- fantry, as usual, showed its superiority over that of the enemy, and was steadily advancing, until the cavalry of Hannibal, returning from the pursuit of the Roman cav- alry, attacked them in the rear. The Roman centre was then broken up, and scattered. Only one division, of 10,000 men, fought its way through the enemy's ranks, and reached Placentia. The rest were mostly killed. The loss of the Carthaginians was quite severe.

The result of the victory of Trebia was the insurrec- tion of all the Celtic tribes in the valley of the Po, who increased Hannibal's army by more than 60,000 infan- try and 4,000 horsemen. The remains of the Roman army wintered in the fortresses of Placentia and Cre- mona. Sempronius managed to escape to Rome.

Hannibal remained where he was for the winter.

No great exertions were made at Rome during this winter for the coming campaign. The consuls, **Gaius Flaminius** and **Gnæus Servilius**, were stationed to guard the two highways leading north from Rome, one of which terminated at **Arretium**, the other at **Arimi- num**. The former was occupied by Flaminius, the latter by Servilius. There they were joined by the troops that had wintered in Placentia and Cremona.

The Romans thought that Hannibal would, of course, march into Central Italy by one of these two highways. The only other route was through Etruria, which in the spring, in the neighborhood of the river Arno, is inundated, and almost impassable. Therefore, the Romans felt safe in this direction. Hannibal, however, determined to take this route, and outflank the enemy. The march through the marshes of Etruria was a hard one. Many men perished; and Hannibal himself lost the use of one eye. He finally arrived at Fæsulæ.

A report of Hannibal's march reached Flaminius at Arretium, who broke up his camp without delay, and endeavored to intercept him. Hannibal, however, had gained a few days' march upon him, and was now near Lake Trasimenus. Here was a narrow defile between two steep mountain walls, closed at its outlet by a high hill, and at its entrance by the lake. Hannibal, with the flower of his infantry, barred the outlet. The light-armed troops and cavalry were drawn up in concealment on either side. The Roman column advanced without hesitation to the unoccupied pass, the thick morning mist concealing from them the position of the enemy. As the head of the Roman line approached the hill at the outlet of the pass, Hannibal gave the signal for battle. The cavalry, advancing behind the heights, closed up the entrance of the pass; and, at the same time, the mist rolled away, and revealed the Phœnician arms on the right and left. It was not a battle, but a mere rout. The main body of the Romans was cut to pieces, with scarcely any resistance; and the consul himself was killed. Fifteen thousand of the Romans fell, and as many more were captured; while the Carthaginians lost but 1,500, most of whom were the Gallic allies of Hannibal. The battle was fought in the early part of the month of May, 217 B.C.

Results. — All Etruria was lost; and Hannibal could

march without hindrance to Rome. The Romans now prepared for the worst. The bridges over the Tiber were broken down. **Quintus Fabius Maximus** was appointed dictator. Hannibal, however, did not march on to Rome, as expected, but directed his course through Umbria, devastating the country as he went. He crossed the Apennines, and halted on the shores of the Adriatic, in **Picenum**. Here he rested some time, to recruit his army after the hardships of the spring campaign. Then he marched slowly along the coast into Southern Italy.

As soon as the Romans found out that Hannibal was not going to attack the city immediately, they raised an army of considerable dimensions, putting it under the command of the same Quintus Fabius Maximus, the dictator. Fabius was a man advanced in years, of determination and firmness. Seeing that Hannibal had come off so easily victorious aforetime, he determined on a new plan of action; viz., to avoid a pitched battle, and follow the Carthaginian army, harassing and keeping it from supplies as far as possible. Hannibal, learning from spies how matters stood, adjusted the plan of his campaign accordingly. Passing the Roman army, he marched over the Apennines again, into the heart of Italy, towards **Beneventum**, and thence to **Capua**, which was the most important of all the Italian cities dependent on Rome. He had formed connections, which led him to hope that it would revolt from Rome on his arrival. During this march of Hannibal, the dictator had followed along the heights, condemning his soldiers to the melancholy task of looking on with arms in their hands; while the Numidian cavalry plundered their faithful allies.

At length, Fabius obtained the opportunity so long looked for by the Roman army of attacking Hannibal. Hannibal, finding that Capua did not open its gates to him, and not being prepared to conduct a siege, commenced his retreat towards the Adriatic. Fabius intercepted his route near **Casilinum**, a town of Campania, on the left bank of the Volturnus. The heights that secured the right bank of the river were occupied by his main army; and the road itself, which led across the river, was guarded by a division of 4,000 men.

Hannibal, however, during the night, ordered his light-armed troops to climb the heights which rose up on the side of the road, and to drive before them a number of oxen with fagots tied to their horns, so that it seemed as if the Carthaginian army was marching off by torchlight. The Roman line, which filled up the road, thinking that they were evaded, and that a further guarding of the road was needless, marched by a side route to the same heights along the road. This left Hannibal's retreat easy. With the bulk of his army, he marched through without encountering the enemy. The next morning, without difficulty, but with severe loss to the Romans, he disengaged and recalled his light-armed troops, which had been sent up to the heights with the oxen.

Hannibal then continued his march, without opposition, in a north-easterly direction, and by a widely circuitous route. He finally arrived, with much booty and a full chest, at Luceria, just as the harvest was about to begin. He encamped and entrenched him-.self at **Geronium**, twenty-five miles north of Luceria, in a plain furnished with grain and grass amply sufficient to support his immense cavalry.

Meanwhile, at Rome, the policy of Fabius was being criticised very severely, — so much so that he was surnamed **Cunctator**, "**the delayer.**" His enemies accused him of cowardice for not attacking Hannibal boldly. It was hard, indeed, for them to see their beautiful fields devastated, without even a show of resistance. In the assembly of the people, the most violent invectives were daily cast at the obstinate old man ; and a resolution was carried to the effect that his command should be shared by one of his lieutenants, Marcus. The army was thus divided into two separate corps ; Marcus at the head of one, intending to attack Hannibal at the first opportunity ; Fabius, at the head of the other, adhering more than ever to his former policy of avoiding a direct battle. Marcus soon found an opportunity, in the open plain of Apulia, of attacking Hannibal ; and, in his impetuosity and want of generalship, his army would have been entirely annihilated, had not the good old Fabius come to his assistance, and helped him withdraw his troops. Then Hannibal spent the winter of 217 and 216 B.C. unmolested.

The Romans had a stormy time at home. They were all determined to resist Hannibal ; but how ? was the question. They saw it would not do to follow the policy of Fabius ; for, if the fields of Italy were devastated for successive seasons, they would be deprived of all means of support. But, on the other hand, whom could they appoint suitable to meet Hannibal in open battle ? He was an enemy truly to be feared ; and they dreaded the shock of arms with him. First, however, they must have an army. After great exertion, they got together 80,000 infantry, one-half allies, and 6,000 cavalry, two-thirds allies, and concluded to put in command of this force **Lucius Æmilius Paulus** and **Caius Terentius Varro**, — names that will go down with all Roman history, as connected with the greatest defeat the Roman arms ever met. Hannibal's army was composed of 10,000 cavalry and 40,000 infantry. He wished for nothing so much as a battle; for he knew that he had never been conquered, and never could be by such men as Paulus and Varro. He was especially desirous of an engagement on this plain, where he could use to advantage his cavalry.

The Romans arrived at Cannæ in June, 216 B.C., and encamped, partly on the right, and partly on the left, bank of the **Aufidus**. The bulk of the Roman army was on the right bank. Early one morning in June, the Romans crossed all their forces to the left bank. The cavalry was stationed on the wings, the right commanded by Paulus, and the left by Varro; in the centre, the infantry, under command of the proconsul, Gnæus Servilius.

Hannibal had drawn up his forces in the form of a crescent, on the left wing his cavalry under **Hasdrubal**, on the right the Numidian horsemen. The battle which followed was a terrible one. The Romans knew that they were fighting for their homes, their wives, their children, every thing they held dear; and, if they were conquered here, their city might become a mere dependant on her rival, Carthage.

Hannibal managed this battle with his usual skill; and the Romans, although double the number of the Carthaginians, were entirely annihilated. Seventy thousand dead were left upon the field. **Paulus** and **Servilius**, and many officers, and 180 men of **Senatorial** rank, were killed.

3*

CHAPTER X.

From Cannæ to Zama.

As soon as the Romans recovered from their first feelings of despair, caused by the defeat of Cannæ, they made the utmost éxertions to raise an army. All the Latin allies were summoned to render aid in the common peril. Boys and old men alike took up arms; and the slaves even were promised freedom if they would join the ranks.

Hannibal, after his brilliant victories, had turned his steps towards Campania, and proceeded to Capua, which he induced to join him before the Romans could send a garrison ; and so this, the second city of Italy, fell into his power. He hoped the smaller cities in the neighborhood would follow the example of Capua, and open their gates to him ; but he was disappointed. The winter of 215–214 B.C. came on, without his having accomplished any thing further; and his army went into winter quarters at Capua. The luxurious habits of the citizens were fraught with danger to the soldiers.

Hannibal saw that, although he had gained so many brilliant victories, he was no nearer the subjugation of Italy than when he entered the basin of the Po. He had expected that the Latin allies of Rome would be dazzled by the brilliancy of his campaigns, and immediately side with him, leaving Rome to fight for herself ; but they had remained true to their allegiance, and, up to this time, Capua was the only city of any importance under the control of Hannibal. It was an

easy thing for him to conquer the Romans on the field
of battle; but his own army must be supported, which
was no easy matter, after having devastated all Italy
from north to south. The Roman granaries, on the
other hand, were kept well supplied from their possessions in Sicily.

Hannibal must therefore bestir himself, and take
some other active means than those already used. Accordingly, he sends to Carthage with an appeal for aid.
He also endeavors to have an alliance formed with
the king of Macedonia, and earnestly urges upon the
commander of the Carthaginians in Spain, Hasdrubal
Barca, to cross the Pyrenees and Alps, and come down
to his assistance; hoping, with this army from the north,
with sustenance and reinforcements from Carthage, and
with such troops as he might obtain from Macedonia,
to concentrate a force around Rome large enough to
compel her into submission.

The Romans realized the position of Hannibal, and
determined to counteract his plans, if possible. Therefore, they kept what troops they could spare in Spain,
under the command of the two Scipios, Publius and
Gnæus, to keep back any forces coming from that quarter to the assistance of Hannibal. They also managed
to keep an army in Northern Greece, to engage the attention of Philip of Macedonia, with whom Hannibal
had formed an alliance.

In Spain, the two Scipios were very successful in
their endeavors to harass the Carthaginian forces, —
in fact, almost dislodge them from the country. But,
when they were on the eve of acquiring this result, the
Carthaginians made a desperate effort; and, by bring-
ing into Spain three armies, managed to separate the

Scipios and their armies, and, surprising them both, not only defeated the armies, but killed both their generals. Thus fell two of the bravest Romans that history has seen.

When this news of the defeat in Spain was received at Rome, it was seen that, unless active measures were taken to check the Carthaginians, they would come down from the Alps, and, uniting with the forces of Hannibal, would place Rome herself in jeopardy. But whom should they send to Spain? No one seemed competent to check these large armies. At last a young man, twenty-seven years old, **Publius Scipio** (whom we first saw at the battle of **Ticinus**), came forward, and said he would undertake the difficult task, and avenge the death of his relatives. It was in 210 B.C. that he set out on this momentous mission; and his appearance on the field of Spain was signalized by a bold and fortunate movement. For early in the spring of 209 B.C., with an army of 30,000 men, he attacked New Carthage, and captured it on the same day. Eighteen vessels of war, 63 transports, $600,000, and 10,000 captives fell into the hands of the Romans. The same year (209 B.C.), Hasdrubal (brother of Hannibal) determined, at any cost, to cross the Pyrenees and Alps with his army, and assist his brother. Scipio endeavored to stop him at a place called Bæcula. Hasdrubal, however, fought his way, step by step, until he reached the Pyrenees. These he crossed. The winter of 209–208 B.C. was spent by him in Gaul.

Two Carthaginian generals were now left in Spain, — Hasdrubal, son of Gisco, and Mago, — who retired, the former to Lusitania, the latter to the Baleares, waiting for reinforcements from Carthage.

The whole east coast of Spain thus fell into the hands of the Romans.

In the year 206 B.C., an army was collected, composed of 32 elephants, 4,000 cavalry, and 70,000 infantry. Scipio met these forces at Bæcula, and thoroughly whipped them.

Hasdrubal and Mago escaped to Gades, which was the only place of all Spain now held by the Carthaginians. Soon after, this place was also abandoned; and the whole of Spain was converted into a Roman province. Scipio now returned to Rome.

In the mean time, in Italy Hannibal had made no permanent progress. In 210 B.C., he lost Capua; and since then had spent his time in Southern Italy, ravaging the country. He took Tarentum, which, however, did not injure the Romans much. In the midst of the difficulties, from which he saw no way of extricating himself without aid, news came that Hasdrubal had crossed the Alps, in the autumn of 208 B.C., and was on his way to meet Hannibal. Hannibal immediately left Southern Italy, and marched up the coast, with the intention of joining his brother. The Romans were very much alarmed, and made strenuous efforts to raise an army large enough to meet the combined forces of Hannibal and Hasdrubal. An army of 40,000 men, under command of G. Nero, hastened north, to intercept Hannibal before he could meet his brother.

Hannibal had followed the coast of the Adriatic north, up through Lucania, into Apulia. The army of Nero, although it managed to intercept that of Hannibal, was unable to stop it; for the Carthaginian, as usual, outgeneralled his adversary. Hannibal proceeded a short distance further, and halted, owing to

some despatches which he had received from Hasdrubal, who wished to join him near this place in Samnium. The Romans, who followed Hannibal closely,
also halted here. Thus the two armies remained inactive some time. Hasdrubal now sent another despatch
to Hannibal, giving further particulars of his route.
These despatches were intercepted by the scouts of the
enemy, and fell into the hands of Nero. By means of
them, Nero found out the exact movements Hasdrubal
proposed to make. He immediately sent forward a
portion of his army for the purpose of intercepting
Hasdrubal, who, abandoned by his guides, lost in a
strange country, and fighting under disadvantages
arising both from his position and ignorance of country,
was himself slain, and his army defeated. The first
intimation Hannibal (who had been waiting anxiously
to hear from Hasdrubal) received of this defeat was
the sight of his brother's head, which was thrown into
the camp by Nero. This defeat occurred in the spring
of 207 B.C., at the Metaurus, a small river south of the
Rubicon, and flowing into the Adriatic. Hannibal
now abandoned Apulia and Lucania, and retired to
Bruttii, where he remained four years.

The Romans determined now to act on the offensive
more than before, and to send an army into Africa,
hoping thereby that Hannibal would be induced to
abandon Italy and protect his own city. Publius Scipio,
who had been so successful in Spain, was put in command of 30,000 men, 40 vessels of war, and 400 transports, and sailed for Africa in the early part of 204 B.C.
Here he was very successful; and, although the Afri-
cans, with the aid of their neighbors, the Numidians,
made strenuous efforts to drive him from their country,

he defeated them with great loss; and the Carthaginians were forced to recall Hannibal from Italy. We can imagine the feelings of the Carthaginian hero, as he left Italy, and the prize which he had coveted so much, and which had been almost within his grasp, not to return in triumph to his native city, but to endeavor to preserve it from that same enemy which he had hoped to have made subject to himself.

He saw, upon his arrival home, that desperate efforts must be made, or Carthage herself would fall into the hands of the Romans. All those capable of bearing arms came forward, and in a short time he had collected a large force. The two armies meet, in the spring of 202 B.C., on the field of Zama, — a name which has been immortalized in history; for it was there that Hannibal met his first and only defeat, and the illustrious P. Scipio won his cognomen of "Africanus." The battle was a hard one; and, after all the newly enrolled troops of Hannibal had been killed or put to flight, his veterans, who had remained by him in Italy, although surrounded on all sides by forces far outnumbering their own, fought on, and were killed one by one around their old chief. The army was fairly annihilated. Hannibal, with only a handful, managed to escape to Hadrumetum. The best parallel of this battle in history is that of Waterloo, where the body-guard of Napoleon fought so desperately around their beloved leader.

With Zama, the Second Punic War closed; and Rome became mistress of the Mediterranean, and of Spain, which she divided into two provinces. Carthage, which had before been her rival, was now merely a defenceless town.

CHAPTER XI.

First and Second Macedonian Wars.

THE overthrow of Carthage, the only power in the West capable of competing with Rome in the career of conquest, left the future mistress of the world in a position to add new nations to her list of subjects.

On the death of Alexander, his vast empire was torn in pieces by his generals; and, after a long and bitter struggle, marked by the blackest crimes, finally resolved itself into the following kingdoms: **Persia**, which continued independent until its overthrow by the Mahometans, long after Rome fell a prey to the barbarians; **Egypt, Syria**, and **Macedon**, which ultimately went to swell the limits of Roman authority.

Egypt owed her decay to the dissensions and weakness of the reigning family rather than to outside influences.

Syria fell, because, composed of various nations which had always enjoyed a sort of semi-independence under the rule of Persia, her encroachments on Egypt and Macedon lessened rather than increased her strength; and, under incompetent rulers, she saw portion after portion of her dominions fall from her, and assume the dignity of new kingdoms. Thus arose **Pergamus, Pontus, Cappadocia, Phrygia**, and other familiar kingdoms.

Macedon never had any stability. Her crown was

a bone of contention from the first ; her people were irritated by the memories of former greatness, jealous of each other and of their new mistress, and constantly striving and plotting for a prominence they had neither the ability to acquire nor the wisdom to maintain.

Thus we see that the East was divided and feeble from intestine wars ; while Rome, in the full tide of victory, was only shaken firmly together by her struggles with Carthage. The memories of one were those of a past influence, a present weakness and decay. Against this, Rome brought the traditions of disasters repaired and overcome, a present full of healthy vigor and hope.

Rome began her interference with the affairs of the East in **Macedon.** Immediately after the battle of Cannæ, **Philip V.**, king of Macedon, sent an embassy to Hannibal, offering him assistance ; but, as the messengers fell into the hands of the Romans, the alliance was not concluded till some years later. Rome sent a small force into Greece, which was soon largely increased by the dissatisfied subjects of Philip.

During this, the **First Macedonian War,** as it is called, **the only object of Rome was to prevent Philip from lending aid to the Carthaginians** ; and in this they were successful.

Philip was not by any means separated from his alliance with Hannibal, as is shown by the fact that he had four thousand men at the battle of Zama. Some of these were made prisoners by the Romans, whom Philip demanded should be returned to him. He received for an answer that, if he wished war, he should have it.

There were several other circumstances which led to

E

the Second Macedonian War (200-197 B.C.). Philip
had made a treaty with Antiochus, king of Syria, for
the partition of Egypt, as soon as the death of Philopater
should place his young son, Epiphanes, on the throne.
The ministers of Egypt at once sought the protection
of Rome; and the envoys who were to assume the office of protectorship remonstrated with Philip on their
journey. In Asia Minor, Philip had conducted himself with such barbarity that the people rose against
him; and Greece was driven from a similar cause to
seek alliances which could protect her against him.
Still Rome was unwilling to undertake a new war;
and the people were induced to vote for it on the
representation that the only means of preventing an
invasion of Italy was to carry the war into Greece
(200 B.C.). The hero of the Second Macedonian War
was T. Quinctius Flaminius, the third leader whom
Rome sent to subdue Philip. After a protracted
struggle, the Macedonians were utterly overthrown at
Cynoscephalæ (197 B.C.), and were then quite ready to
listen to reason. The terms of the peace were the same
as had been offered early in the war: Philip was to
withdraw his garrisons from all the Grecian cities,
leave them independent for the future, make reparation
for past injuries, and pay a sum of money. The Greeks
were dismayed at the mildness shown; but the Romans
tempered their victories with wisdom, and were of no
mind to give up their hold on Greece by removing
Philip, the cause of their interference. The Senate
confirmed the terms of peace; and, after putting the
affairs of the country in order, Flaminius, contrary to
all expectation, restored liberty to Greece, removing
all the Roman garrisons, and urging the people to

"show themselves worthy of the gift of the Roman people," and returned home to receive a glorious triumph. The results of the war were the overthrow of every controlling influence in Greece, and the establishing of a de facto Roman protectorate. The last trace of domestic unity was destroyed by the practical dissolution of the famous Achæan League, whose members were so divided on the question of which side they should espouse in the conflict that its authority was destroyed. In addition to this, the wedge had been entered, and the interference of Rome in eastern affairs was assured ; also two of the divisions of the empire of Alexander, Greece and Egypt, were under the immediate protection of Rome, so that the débris of Syria were alone independent.

CHAPTER XII.

THE SYRIAN WAR.

ANTIOCHUS, king of Syria, showed no disposition to listen to the remonstrance of Flaminius, but crossed the Hellespont, and thus brought himself in collision with Rome. This is one of the junctures in history at which we are prone to pause, and consider what might have been. Hannibal, fleeing from home, escaped to Ephesus, the seat of the Syrian court, and offered the monarch every inducement to go to war with Rome. His counsels were listened to only so far as the raising of an army and the invading of Greece. Much time was wasted in idleness; and, after an unsuccessful attempt to hold the pass of Thermopylæ, which terminated in utter defeat, he fled back into Asia. **Lucius Scipio** was placed in command of the Roman forces destined to the invasion of Asia, and at once hastened to the scene of action. Antiochus raised an immense army, with which he hoped to crush the invaders; but he met with disaster from the first. Hannibal's Phœnician fleet was overthrown and dispersed by the Rhodians; and the war was terminated by a crushing defeat at **Magnesia** (190 B.C.), where 53,000 of the Syrian army were left dead on the field, the Roman loss amounting to but 400 men. Scipio returned to Rome to enjoy his triumph, and added **Asiaticus** to his name, as his brother had taken that of **Africanus**, in commemoration of his victory.

The successor of Scipio in the East, **Cn. Manlius Vulso,** found nothing to do which could add to his renown. So he marched against the Gauls, who had settled in **Galatia** about a century before, and had become very wealthy from continual plunderings. The **excuse** for the attack was that they had served in the army of Antiochus; the **reason** was their wealth, and the ambition of the consul for glory. They were easily overthrown, their wealth was seized, and they themselves speedily became assimilated to their neighbors. The possessions of Antiochus in Asia Minor were distributed among the allies of Rome.

The most marked **result** of the Syrian war was the introduction into Rome of immense wealth, which laid the foundation of the Oriental extravagance and luxury which finally undermined the integrity of the state. From Greece were brought learning and refinement; from Asia, immorality and effeminacy. The rigor and tone of Roman society are nowhere more forcibly shown than in the length of time it took for its subjugation by these ruinous exotics.

Another innovation was at this time introduced into the conduct of war by the Roman generals; for the conquest of the Galatians was the first instance in which the authority of the Senate had been dispensed with in making war; and the triumph which rewarded its success stamped it as legal, and made it a precedent which was afterwards but too frequently taken advantage of.

CHAPTER XIII.

Third Macedonian War (171–168 B.C.).

Philip was now subjugated. Still his ambition would not let him rest. He placed both his finances and his army on the best footing possible, and soon began to enlarge his boundaries. Complaints were made at Rome; and his son, Demetrius, was sent thither as an hostage, and to offer explanations. The mind of the king was poisoned against this son by **Perseus** (Perses), his half-brother; and Demetrius was put to death by the command of Philip, on a charge of treason (179 B.C.). The discovery of the fraud weighed on the king's mind, so that he died soon after; and Perseus reaped the reward of his villany.

At first, the new monarch made good use of his opportunities, and soon offended the Senate by his interference in the affairs of Greece. War was declared (171 B.C.); but the forces sent by Rome were no match for the excellent army of the Macedonians; and nothing was gained until **L. Æmilius Paulus** was made consul, and took charge of the war (168 B.C.). A single battle, at **Pydna** (June 22), annihilated the army of Perseus; and the king fled to Samothrace with his treasures and his family. He was taken, brought to Rome, and served to adorn the triumph of his conqueror. The Macedonian monarchy ceased to exist. Perseus died soon after; and his son became a clerk in Rome. The

Romanizing of Greece was complete. By separating the country into four independent republics, whose members could not intermarry or trade with each other, utter demoralization soon ensued, and proved a certain preventive to all alliances which could shake the authority of the conqueror. Once, indeed, under the leadership of Pseudo-Philip, who pretended (148 B.C.) to be the son of Philip V., the Macedonians showed signs of disaffection ; but Macedon fell without a struggle, and was soon formed into a Roman province. In 146 B.C., Greece fell with the capture of Corinth by Mummius, and was also formed into a province, under the name of Achaia.

CHAPTER XIV.

CARTHAGE BETWEEN THE SECOND AND THIRD PUNIC WARS. — HER FALL.

FIFTY years intervened between the Second and Third Punic Wars.

This was a period of great **commercial** prosperity for Carthage; but her government was weak, being continually divided into factions, each working for its own interests.

Masinissa, king of the Numidians (a people neighboring to the Carthaginians), an ally of Rome, was bitterly complained of by Carthage to Rome. He snatched from her one district after another. Carthage, bound by her treaty with Rome not to undertake any war without her sanction, was obliged first to complain to Rome.

The Romans, for appearance' sake, sent over some persons to act as mediators between Carthage and Masinissa. But these commissioners did not bring any thing to a decision. They allowed things to go on as they might, without pronouncing a sentence either one way or the other. At last, a war broke out between the Carthaginians and Masinissa. The latter was victorious. The Carthaginian army surrendered their arms; the best part of their territory was given up, and Carthage had to pay $5,000,000.

The Romans had, as usual, sent commissioners, who, with a truly diabolic spirit, deferred giving any deci-

sion, but instigated Masinissa. They sent their reports
to Rome, informing the Senate of the great resources
which Carthage still possessed. It was at this time
that **Cato** kept reiterating in the Senate his famous
sentence, **" Delenda est Carthago,"** — **" Carthage must
be destroyed."**

After the victory of Masinissa, things came to a
crisis. The Romans, imagining that it was an easy
affair, determined upon the destruction of Carthage.

The Carthaginians were called upon to give an account for their conduct towards the Numidian king.
Desponding and broken-hearted, they sent ambassadors
to Rome. The answer there given them was obscure.
They were requested to make reparation to Rome ;
but, at the same time, they were assured that nothing
should be undertaken against Carthage herself. But,
in 149 B.C., the consuls, **Manius Manilius** and **Lucius
Marcius Censorinus**, led an army, consisting, it is said,
of 80,000 foot and 4,000 horse to Sicily, where the
troops were organized, and other Carthaginian ambassadors waited for.

When they appeared, the consuls declared that the
Senate did not wish to encroach upon the freedom of
the Carthaginian people ; but, as they were divided
into so many parties, it desired to have some security ;
and for this purpose it demanded that, within thirty
days, 300 children of the noblest Carthaginian families
should be delivered up into their hands as hostages.

These children were sent over to Sicily by their
parents, in heart-rending despair.

After the Romans had, in this manner, secured the
submission of Carthage, their army crossed over to
Africa. The Roman consuls now informed the Car-

4

thaginians that they were ready to treat with them on any thing that had not been previously settled.

When the Carthaginian ambassadors appeared before the consuls, they were told that Carthage must deliver up all her arms and artillery ; for they said, as Rome was able to protect her, there was no reason for Carthage to possess arms. Hard as this command was, it was obeyed; and the Carthaginians now believed that they had satisfied the Romans in every respect. But, when they had their last audience, they were told that the government of Carthage had indeed shown its good will, but that Rome had no control over the city so long as it was fortified. The preservation of peace, therefore, required that the people should quit the city, give up their navy, and build a new town, without walls, at a distance of ten miles from the sea-coast.

The indignation and fury which this demand excited in Carthage were so great, that all the gates were instantly closed ; and all the Romans and Italians who happened to be within the city were massacred.

The consuls imagined that Carthage might be taken by storm in an instant. The city, situated on a peninsula, was protected on one side by a treble wall; but on the side towards the Bay of Tunis it had only one low wall. The Romans, who expected to find a defenceless population, attempted to storm both walls. But despair had suggested to the Carthaginians means of defence on both sides ; and they repelled the assault. Everybody was engaged, day and night, in the manufacture of arms.

The result of the war was not decided until four years after its commencement. The history of it is very distressing. There can be nothing more heart-rending than this last struggle of despair, which was necessary, and yet could not end otherwise than in the destruction of Carthage.

Two years after the war began, **Publius Cornelius Scipio** was made consul. He was the son of **Æmilius Paulus**, the hero of **Pydna**, and the adopted son of Cornelius Scipio, the son of the conqueror of Hannibal. This Scipio was truly a very eminent general and a great man, but a strong conservative, persisting in upholding the actual state of things, no matter in how deplorable a condition they might be.

Scipio began to besiege Carthage with all his energy. He stopped up the mouth of the harbor, and finally got within the walls of the city. The houses were conquered one by one, by breaking through the walls from room to room and from house to house. The struggle was, at the same time, carried on upon the flat roofs of the houses. A complete famine raged in the city; and the living fed upon the bodies of the dead.

During this unspeakable misery, the Romans gradually advanced to the highest part of the city, which they finally took. Thus Carthage fell (146 B.C.), and her destruction was complete. A part of her territory was given to Numidia, and the rest made a Roman province, called **Africa**.

CHAPTER XV.

ROME AND SPAIN.

ROME formed her possessions in Spain into **two** provinces shortly after the Second Punic War (198 B.C.). This was followed by a general rising of the Spaniards, doubtless from fear that a conquest of the entire country was intended ; but they were speedily repressed by the consul, **M. Portius Cato** (195 B.C.), who exhibited genuine Roman energy in their subjection, and Roman ferocity in their punishment. A desultory struggle, however, soon arose, which was terminated (179 B.C.), after sixteen years, by the more moderate measures of **Tib. Sempronius Gracchus.** The Spaniards bound themselves to pay certain yearly dues to the Senate, and not to fortify any city without its consent.

The rapacity of the governors led to much complaint ; and, finally, the inhabitants of the town of **Segeda**, on the Tagus, entered into an alliance with the Numantines, who lived further up the river, and began to rebuild their walls. Several commanders were sent against them, and **Lucullus** compelled them to sue for peace ; but the Senate refused to grant terms, and the war continued.

At the same time, the Lusitanian shepherds made frequent inroads on the further province, which the prætor Galba endeavored to repress, but was defeated, and barely escaped with a few horse. The next year, he forced them to make submission, but, receiving them with pretended kindness, ordered them to meet him in three bodies, at different places, and, when they came, fell upon them, and massacred them. **Viriathus** then took command of the Lusitanians who had escaped ; and for several years his successes were only interrupted during the brief command of **Metellus Macedonicus**; for, when he was succeeded by Q. Pompeius, matters returned to their former state.

The consul **Mancinus** (137 B.C.) was obliged to capitulate, and, to save himself and his army, made a treaty, which the Senate refused to sanction ; and Mancinus was delivered up to the enemy, as Postumius had been surrendered to the Sabines; but the Spaniards, like the Sabines, refused to accept him as a substitute for the fulfilment of the treaty.

Viriathus was assassinated soon after, and his people were then subdued ; and the pacification was ably conducted by **Dec. Junius Brutus** (138 B.C.). The Numantine War continued, until by the strictest blockade, under Scipio, the inhabitants of the town of Numantia were reduced to the verge of starvation ; and then, only, they surrendered (133 B.C.). The town was so effectually destroyed that even its site cannot be discovered. Scipio added to his name "**Numantinus**," in honor of the conquest.

CHAPTER XVI.

THE GRACCHI.

WHILE the Numantine War was still in progress, the slaves in Sicily broke into rebellion; and their numbers increased so rapidly that it was five years before they could be subdued.

For a long time, slave labor had been taking the place of that of freemen. The supply was rendered enormous by constant wars, and by regular slave-trade carried on with the shores of the Black Sea and Greece. The owners of the slaves became an idle aristocracy, rendered so by their perfect immunity from labor. They were jealous of each other and of the more powerful classes of the state; and, having full leisure to shape their discontents into action, they only needed a leader to divide the Roman Empire against itself.

The steady growth of the power of the people encouraged still further encroachments on the prerogatives of the senatorial class; so that every thing was ripe, on the advent of Tiberius Gracchus, for the arraying of the people against the Senate, thus ushering in the contest which only ended with the Republic, and brought to the surface some of the proudest names of Roman history.

On one side or the other, we find them — Marius and Sulla, Pompey and Cæsar, Antony and Augustus — arraying Rome against herself, till the glories of the republic were swallowed up·in the misrule and dishonor of the empire.

Tiberius Gracchus, immediately on his election as tribune, set about reforming the abuses which had crept into the state; but he did this in a manner so peremptory and violent as to deprive his efforts of all their effect. He proposed to limit the amount of public lands any head of a family could own to five hundred jugera (about 320 acres). This was a direct blow at the wealthy classes, as they naturally had obtained possession of the greater portion of the lands. Another tribune was induced to veto the bill; and Gracchus immediately procured the deposition of his adversary, after which the law was passed.

Having injured his popularity by his indiscretion, he sought to regain it by presenting laws certain of popular approval. The term of military service was to be shortened; jurors were to be chosen from all owning a certain amount of property, not from the senators only; and an appeal was to be established from the courts to the assembly of the people. These reforms enabled him to obtain a second election, which was claimed to be illegal; and, to prevent his profiting by it, he was murdered, with some three hundred of his followers, in a brawl.

Thus was shed the first blood of the Civil War (B.C. 133). His mantle fell to his brother Caius Gracchus, who persisted in the course laid out by Tiberius. He also endeavored to admit all the Italians to the privileges of Roman citizenship, and to limit the price of bread, as a means of increasing his popularity. Against the Senate he established the first permanent court of justice in Rome, — that for trying the cases of provincial magistrates accused of corrupt dealings in their government. He took all judicial power from the Senate's hands, and gave it to a council; deprived it of its supervision of public roads, and the apportionment of the provinces between the consuls.

The enlargement of the privileges of the Italians ruined the popularity of Caius Gracchus; and (121 B.C.), like his brother, he fell in a riot. By his death, the senatorial party recovered somewhat of their authority; but the fierceness with which party strife raged made the people eager to accept the rule of any one who should have the ability to control the factions of the state.

This man was found in Caius Marius, born at Arpinum, whose sole recommendations were that he was inflexible in his determination, and an excellent soldier. He sprung from an old, though rustic family; contemned the polite education of the times; was very superstitious; and always accompanied by a Syrian prophetess, in whose counsels he had implicit faith. He flattered the populace, and delighted to appear among them as an equal. He possessed great wealth, acquired in war, and was considered a man of incorruptible integrity. His talents as a general were marked. He had few friends; for the prominent features of his character were bitterness, hatefulness, and cruelty. But he was, at the same time, the man to save Rome, the degradation of which had been brought about by those who opposed him. At the siege of Numantia, in Spain, Scipio had noticed the courage of Marius, and predicted a brilliant career for him.

In 119 B.C., he obtained the office of tribune; two years later, that of prætor. Not long after, he married the great-aunt of Cæsar, **Julia**. He then went to Numidia, as lieutenant of Metellus, to assist in conducting the war against Jugurtha.

The foreign wars during this period were important. The **Balearic** Isles, **Pergamus**, and **Dalmatia** were added to the Roman empire. But by far the most important war was that against **Jugurtha** (118–104 B.C.).

After the destruction of Carthage, the most important kingdom in Africa was Numidia, which contained numerous and flourishing cities, the centres of great commerce.

Upon the death of Masinissa, the kingdom had been divided among his three sons, two of whom soon died, leaving the government wholly in the hands of **Micipsa**, the surviving son. He had two sons, between whom he intended to divide the kingdom. With these two sons, he had educated also a natural son of one of his deceased brothers, named **Jugurtha**, who was adopted by Micipsa, and shared with his two cousins the kingdom at Micipsa's death (118 B.C.).

Jugurtha was very talented, but bold, cunning, and adroit. He had no idea of the sanctity of an oath, no honesty, and no humanity. He soon quarrelled with his cousins, murdered one, and compelled the other to flee. The exile went to Rome, and there pleaded his case. Jugurtha hastened also to Rome, to convince the Senate with what had now become the weightiest of arguments, **gold**, of the propriety of his conduct.

The Senate was purchased, and decreed that Numidia should be divided between Jugurtha and the fugitive.

Jugurtha now made war on his cousin, and, gaining possession of his person, put him to death.

Again Rome interfered, and again the **Senate** was bought off; but the **people** refused to make any terms with the murderer, and war was declared with Jugurtha.

The conduct of the war fell, after some reverses, to Metellus (109 B.C.), who restored the discipline of the army, and drove Jugurtha from his throne. In this he was ably seconded by Marius, who was at this time about fifty years old.

During this war, Marius returned to Rome, and obtained the office of consul (107 B.C.); and also received the command to bring the war against Jugurtha to a close. Metellus retired to Rome in disgust. It required two campaigns for Marius to conclude the war.

The capture of Jugurtha was directly due to **Lucius Cornelius Sulla** (Sylla), who delivered him to Marius, but claimed all the honor of the exploit.

In 104 B.C., Marius returned to Rome, and entered the city in triumph. Jugurtha was thrown into a dungeon, and there starved to death.

CHAPTER XVII.

THE CIMBRI AND TEUTONES. — THE SOCIAL WAR.

THE war against Jugurtha was thus concluded, and it was none too soon ; for Rome required the talents of Marius in a war compared with which that against the Numidian king was insignificant.

The Cimbri and Teutones, races from Northern Europe, were threatening the frontiers of Italy. The Roman armies had been annihilated by these barbarians a short time previous to this (106 B.C.), on the banks of the Rhone.

Marius, now the only man on whom the nation fixed its hopes, was made consul for a second time (104 B.C.).

The barbarians, after their victory on the Rhone, had fortunately turned to Spain, and spent a few years in roaming over and laying waste that country.

Marius now devoted his energies to forming and training a new army.

The elements of which the Roman armies had formerly consisted had degenerated of late years. The task of Marius to make well-disciplined soldiers out of the material he had on hand was a difficult one. He chose the field on the banks of the Rhone, in the southern part of Gaul, as the best for exercising his troops. Here he accustomed them to the greatest possible exertions. Many perished under the hardships ; but those who survived became hardened soldiers. At length, in his fourth consulship (102 B.C.), he marched against the enemy.

When the barbarians returned from Spain (102 B.C.), they separated their forces, the Cimbri marching around the northern foot of the Alps towards Noricum, with the intention of invading Italy from that quarter, the Teutones remaining in Gaul.

Marius finally came to an engagement with the Teutones in the neighborhood of Aquæ Sextiæ (Aix), in the summer of 102 B.C. The battle raged for two days, and ended in the utter defeat of the barbarians. Those who survived the battle put an end to themselves of their own accord.

The Cimbri, in the mean while, had crossed the Alps, and were ravaging the fertile fields of Lombardy, meeting with but little opposition by Catulus, the other consul.

The next year, Marius, now consul for the fifth time, joined Catulus, and won a decisive victory near Vercellæ. The fate of the Cimbri was the same as that of the Teutones. The victories of Aquæ Sextiæ and Vercellæ raised Marius to a dangerous eminence.

Never, since the establishment of the republic, had a single citizen so far outshone all rivals.

Had Marius possessed real statesmanship, he might have anticipated the work of Julius Cæsar, and have become the permanent head of the state. But, though sufficiently ambitious, he lacked judgment and firmness. He had no clear and definite views, either of the exact position to which he aspired, or of the means whereby he was to attain it. His course was marked by hesitation and indecision. Endeavoring to please all parties, he pleased none. At first, he gave his sanc-

tion to a long series of measures which aimed at securing the favor of the lower orders.

It is hard to give a clear account of what happened
at Rome at this time. Marius formed connections with
two rascals, Apuleius Saturninus and Servilius Glaucia.
The former, a plebeian by birth, an eloquent speaker,
and bitter enemy of the Senate, was appointed tribune of
the people ; the latter, of noble origin, was chosen prætor. Their election was stained by the murder of one
Nonius, who was a competitor of Saturninus for the
tribuneship.

Saturninus caused to be passed some agrarian laws,
which granted (1) to the poor citizens all the country
which had been occupied by the Cimbri in the northern
part of Italy, north of the Po ; (2) one hundred acres
of land in Africa to the veterans of Marius.

The Senate refused at first to sanction these laws,
but afterwards consented, except Metellus Numidicus,
who was exiled for his refusal.

At the next consular elections, riots occurred. The
Senate declared Saturninus and Glaucia public enemies,
and thereupon seized the capitol.

Marius, seeing his associates likely to be worsted,
deserted them. They were seized, and put to death.

The fall of Saturninus was followed (99 b.c.) by the
recall of Metellus from banishment, and the voluntary
exile of the haughty and now generally unpopular
Marius. That great general, but poor statesman, retired
to Asia, and visited the court of Mithridates, king of
Pontus. For the next eight years (99–91 b.c.), Rome
enjoyed a season of comparative quiet.

Livius Drusus, of noble birth and large fortune, a
thorough aristocrat, full of energy and pride, when

elected tribune undertook to conciliate the people by the redivision of lands, and the distribution of wheat, and the admittance of the Italians to the rights of Roman citizenship.

But the Roman conservatives violently opposed him, and finally had him assassinated (91 B.C.).

The death of Drusus drove the Italians to despair; and, finding their champion murdered, and their hopes dashed to the ground, they rose in arms. Eight nations entered into close alliance, chose Corfinium, in the Pelignian Apennines, for their capital, and formed a federal republic, to which they gave the name of Italia.

This war, called the Social War (90–88 B.C.), *i.e.* war of the allies, was at first attended with great success. The allies overran Campania, defeated the Romans a number of times, and entered into negotiations with the Northern Italians, whose fidelity began to waver.

Rome, seeing that she could not subdue the rebellion by force of arms, determined to make concessions, and, by the Julian and Plotian laws, granted to the Italians all that they ever demanded.

CHAPTER XVIII.

MARIUS AND SULLA.

WITH the name of Marius is usually coupled that of Sulla, who was over twenty years his junior. Sulla and Marius were men of two different generations; and this circumstance added to the aversion which existed between them. While the former was of noble birth, the latter was a soldier, who had risen by his talents and fortune.

In the Jugurthine war, Sulla had been quæstor of Marius, and had taken a prominent part in the capture of the king. Fortune accompanied him everywhere; and it was this good fortune that drew the attention of the people towards him. Marius acquired great merits in the Social War; but Sulla eclipsed his fame. Marius was under the influence of the sad feeling — which must be particularly painful to an old man — that the rising sun outshone him, and made him invisible. Sulla thus called forth in Marius a spirit of opposition.

Marius, who was insatiable in his ambition and love of power, was now anxious to obtain the command of the war against Mithridates, king of Pontus. But the Senate gave the command to Sulla. Marius, impelled by his irresistible desire to humble his adversary, induced the tribune, Publius Sulpicius, to make a plebis-citum (i.e. a law passed by the comitia tributa, at the motion of the tribune), by which the command was taken from Sulla. 'Sulla was naturally exasperated at this unjustifiable course, and immediately marched to Rome at the head of six legions, compelling Marius to leave the city. He fled to **Ostia**, and from there along the coast to **Minturnæ**, from which place he sailed to Africa, where for a time he lived quietly, watching the course of events.

Meanwhile, at Rome, Sulla proscribed his enemies, repealed the bill of Sulpicius, and put Sulpicius himself to death. But he could not remain long at the capital. The affairs of the East called him away; and no sooner was he gone than the flames of civil war burst out afresh.

A man named **Cinna** now came forward as the head of the party of Marius. He recalled the aged exile; and, supported by the Italians, marched upon Rome. The city was captured. Marius caused himself to be made consul the **seventh** time (January, 86 B.C.), and Cinna the **second**. The victory thus gained was followed by the wildest cruelties. Marius had a bodyguard of slaves, whom he sent out to murder those whom he wished to get rid of. The houses of the rich were plundered; and the honor of the noble families exposed to the mercy of slaves. But the death of Marius, sixteen days after he entered upon his consulship, put an end to the shedding of blood, but not to the bitter party spirit.

During the three years which followed the death of Marius, Sulla was conducting the war against Mithridates in Achaia and Asia, and Italy was completely under control of the party of Cinna.

In 84 B.C., Cinna himself was murdered, when on the eve of setting out against Sulla in Asia.

CHAPTER XIX.

The Mithridatic War.

The kingdom of Pontus, an offshoot of Persia, was founded by Ariobarzanes I. in 363 B.C. Six kings of little note followed him, until, in 120 B.C., Mithridates VI., surnamed the "Great," ascended the throne. He was yet a minor when his father died. But he employed his time well in training both his mind and body, — the former, by the study of languages, of which he is said to have spoken twenty-five; the latter, by perpetual hunting expeditions in the roughest and most remote regions.

On reaching the age of twenty, he endeavored to extend his dominions, wherever he could, without coming in contact with the Romans. In the short space of seven years, he added to his kingdom Lesser Armenia, Colchis, the entire eastern coast of the Black Sea, the Chersonesus Taurica (Crimea).

Mithridates first came in contact with the Romans as follows : —

The family of the kings of Cappadocia had become extinct, and Mithridates gave the throne to his brother ; but the Romans set up an opposing king against him.

Nicomedes, king of Bithynia, was also incited by the Romans to attack the king of Pontus, but was defeated ; and his own brother was set up against him by Mithridates.

The Romans now openly interfered, and spoke to Mithridates in a tone as if he had been the offender. Nothing could be more unjust. They collected three armies against him (composed chiefly of effeminate inhabitants of Asia Minor), which were easily defeated by the well-disciplined troops of Mithridates.

The whole of Asia Minor soon recognized Mithridates as their sovereign. This induced him to cross over into Greece, where he was received with universal joy; and nearly the whole of Greece submitted to him.

Most of the Greek towns in Lydia and Caria were provoked by the Romans; and, being encouraged by Mithridates, put to death on one day some 80,000 Romans. This act demanded vengeance, and called forth the utmost exertions on the part of the Romans.

The Senate, as we have seen, gave the command to Sulla, 87 B.C. The same year, Sulla went to Thessaly.

Archelaus, the general of Mithridates, held possession of Greece. Sulla met his forces on the field of **Chæroneia**, 86 B.C., and totally defeated them. He then attacked Athens, which was occupied by a Pontic garrison, and, after a long siege, captured the city, and thus obtained control of the whole of Greece.

Sulla then concluded a peace with Mithridates on these conditions: The king was to give up Bithynia, Paphlagonia, and Cappadocia, and withdraw to his former dominions. He was also to pay a sum of $2,000,-000, and surrender 70 ships of war.

Having thus settled matters in Asia Minor, and punished the Lydians and Carians, in whose dominions the Romans had been massacred, by compelling them to pay at once five years' tribute, Sulla was ready to return to

Rome.   But this was an undertaking of no ⌐
portions.

The Marian faction had at their disposal an army o.
nearly 200,000 men, ready to repel Sulla as soon as he
attempted to land on his native shores.

CHAPTER XX.

SULLA IN ITALY. — SERTORIUS IN SPAIN. — SPARTACUS.

SULLA had early announced his intention of punishing his enemies in Italy; and every preparation was made by the Marian party for his reception. An attempt was made to win the people by means of the ever popular agrarian law, and the extension of the franchise; but no sooner did Sulla land in Italy (83 B.C.) than the soldiers were induced to desert in immense numbers; and, what with incapacity on the one hand and bribery on the other, Sulla soon found himself in possession of all lower Italy.

Among those who hastened to the standard of Sulla was young Cn. Pompey, then but twenty-three years old, who was destined to become a great man at a time when great men were plenty. It was to his efforts that Sulla's success was largely due. The next year, the Marian party was joined by the Samnites; and war raged hotter than ever. At length, however, Sulla was victorious under the walls of Rome; and the city lay at his mercy. His first act, an order for the slaughter of 6,000 Samnite prisoners, whom he had taken, was a fit prelude to his conduct in the city. Every effort was made to eradicate the last trace of Marian blood and sympathy from Italy. Citizens were placed on the proscription lists, which condemned them to death, and their property to be sold. To what extent this was carried, we may learn from the fact that nearly 5,000 persons are said to have lost their lives in this manner. The sales of confiscated property were carried on under the eye of the conqueror, and the proceeds were disposed of at his caprice. After annihilating the popular party, and enacting a series of laws **re-establishing the supremacy of the Senate**, Sulla retired, content with a single term as consul, to a country seat, where he abandoned himself to every species of debauchery, and died a miserable death after about a year (79 B.C.).

He had quieted the contentions of the state by murdering all who opposed him. As in all measures of unrestrained violence some fatal error undoes the work intended, so Sulla, by ill-judged clemency, permitted the escape of one whose fame was destined to eclipse his own, and who finally overthrew both the Senate and the people. This was **C. Julius Cæsar**, son-in-law to Cinna, and nephew to Marius. When Sulla ordered all to divorce their wives of Marian lineage, Cæsar refused, and was permitted to escape.

On the death of Sulla, **Crassus** and **M. Æmilius Lepidus** were chosen consuls; but such was the instability of the times, that they were sworn not to raise an army during their consulship. Lepidus attempted to evade his oath by going to Gaul; and, when ordered by the Senate to return, he marched at the head of his forces. He was defeated (78 B.C.) near the city by Crassus and Pompey, and soon after died.

In Spain, affairs were as bad as possible. **Quintus Sertorius**, a partisan of Marius, had escaped (83 B.C.) thither during the proscription of Sulla, and by his talents and ability had united the Spaniards and Marian refugees under his standard (78 B.C.).   Success followed him, and with it popularity, till finally the Romans in Spain became jealous of the favors bestowed on the Spaniards, and created a faction.   Both **Metellus** and **Pompey** were sent against him ; but, owing to their mutual jealousy, the rebel held his ground.   Sertorius was not proof against the temptations of prosperity, and began to conspire to reinstate his party (the Marians) in power at Rome.   **Perperna,** who had been a general under Lepidus, after his commander's defeat (*cf.* page 93), fled to Sertorius with the remnant of his army ; and, imagining that he might supplant Sertorius in popularity, caused him to be assassinated.   With the death of Sertorius fell the Marian party in Spain (72 B.C.).

At the same time, a still more dangerous enemy was threatening Italy.   At Capua, a band of gladiators, under the leadership of one of their number, named **Spartacus,** escaped (73 B.C.) from the training school, and took up a strong position on Mt. Vesuvius.   They were joined by large numbers of slaves and outcasts of every description, and were soon in a position to defeat two prætors who were sent against them.   The next year, they assumed the offensive ; and Spartacus found himself at the head of 100,000 men.   Four generals sent against him were defeated ; and, for two years, he ravaged Italy as he pleased, and even threatened Rome. But intestine division showed itself in his ranks : his lieutenants grew jealous of him.

In 71 B.C., the command of the war was given to **Crassus** (the same who won the battle before Rome for Sulla), who finished it in six months.   Spartacus fell fighting bravely near Brundisium.

Pompey, returning from the Sertorian war in Spain, met 5,000 of those who had escaped from the army of Spartacus, whom he slew to a man. Crassus pointed the moral of his victory by hanging 6,000 captives, whom he had taken along the road from Rome to Capua (72 B.C.).

CHAPTER XXI.

POMPEY AND CRASSUS. — MITHRIDATIC WAR.

POMPEY and Crassus both put themselves forward for the consulship; and, though neither was eligible according to law, both were elected (70 B.C.). Reforms were immediately begun ; the legislation of Sulla was undermined; and the power of the nobles received a check from which it never after recovered.

No good could be hoped from the union of Crassus with Pompey; for each was mortally jealous of the other, and each retained his army near Rome. Neither, fortunately, desired to proceed to blows. Pompey's popularity soon began to wane ; for, though naturally allied to the senatorial party, he endeavored to lead that of the people. Thus he lost the confidence of the one, without gaining that of the other. At this time, affairs in the East brought him again prominently to favor.

Mithridates, taking advantage of the trouble at Rome, was again in arms. Lucullus was sent (74 B.C.) against him, and was everywhere successful ; but one of his generals risked an unfortunate battle, and was defeated (67 B.C.). The army now mutinied, and refused to march further eastward. Thus he was compelled to suspend operations ; and, before they could be renewed, the command had passed (66 B.C.) to Pompey.

Pompey earned his appointment to the East by his

successes against the **Greek pirates**. From the earliest times, these marauders had been in the habit of depredating on the shores of the Mediterranean. During the civil wars of Rome, they had become much bolder; so that the city was compelled to take an active part against them. Pompey was placed in charge (67 B.C.) of the undertaking, and in **three months** the pirates were swept from the sea; and he was now named as the man to conclude the Mithridatic war. His appointment was violently opposed by the Senate; but Cicero came to his assistance with his first political speech (**Pro lege Manilia**). The command was at once given to him; and he became virtually dictator in the East.

Pompey went to Asia, speedily drove Mithridates from his kingdom, and converted Syria to a Roman province. At this time, he was invited to act as judge between two aspirants to the Jewish throne, and, his decision being contrary to the desires of the people, led his army against Jerusalem, which he captured after a siege of three months, and installed his *protégé* on the throne on condition of an annual tribute. Mithridates now returned to Pontus for the prosecution of his old design; but so great was the terror inspired by the Roman arms, that even his own son refused to join him. Desperate at the turn affairs had taken, the aged monarch put an end to his own life (63 B.C.); and with him ended the last formidable opposition to Rome in Asia for many years. After an absence of nearly seven years, Pompey returned to Rome, and received a well-earned triumph.

CHAPTER XXII.

Conspiracy of Catiline.

While Pompey was absent in the East, matters at Rome were daily becoming worse, and shaping themselves for the speedy overthrow of the republic. There were many who had suffered under Sulla, and who were anxious to regain what they had lost; and there were many who, enriched by the dictator, had squandered their ill-gotten wealth, and now only waited a leader to renew the assault upon the state. The Senate was alarmed at the power of the people; and the people distrusted the Senate. One of the creations of the time was **L. Sergius Catiline**, a man of immense strength and courage, of good manners, and with all the attributes for popularity both with the army and the people, but with a character utterly devoid of honesty, virtue, or patriotism. Disappointed in his hope of obtaining the consulship, he formed (65 B.C.) a plot to murder the consuls, and seize their offices. The scheme failed, the signal for the attack being prematurely given; yet, though the guilt of Catiline was beyond doubt, he not only escaped punishment, but became a formidable candidate for the consulship two years later (63 B.C.), when Cicero was elected. Catiline then entered into a new plot, which added to the designs of the former the burning of the city. This conspiracy was discovered by Cicero, and became the occasion of his four orations against Catiline. The masterspirit was even then allowed to escape; indeed, so weak were the authorities, that his departure from Rome was the one thing they most desired. Others of the conspirators were arrested, and the great danger was passed; for Catiline and his small army were of little importance in the field, however dangerous they might be in the city. A serious difficulty now arose as to the disposition to be made of the prisoners. **Cato** and **Cicero** advocated their being put to death; while **Cæsar** opposed to this imprisonment for life. The motives of the men are so characteristic that they form a complete key to their several public careers. **Cicero**, vain and selfish, weak in council, and distrustful of the temper of the people and his own ability to rule their factions, feared lest they become dangerous enemies to himself: **Cato**, desiring the reformation of the state, would have made them an example and warning for the future. The one, forgetful of the state, was overcome by personal fears: the other, unmindful of self, would have purity at any cost. **Cæsar**, careless alike of danger and reform, would have every thing done in strict accordance with the laws; and, a bold and wise statesman, urged that nothing was more impolitic than lawless violence on the part of rulers. On the one hand, we have the timid magistrate and the injudicious reformer: on the other, the statesman and politician, with less integrity of purpose, perhaps, than the one, less disinterested patriotism than the other, but, with keener knowledge and a stronger hand, a far safer guide. A sentence of death was voted; and Cicero, with unseemly haste, caused the conspirators to be executed that very night.

Catiline was defeated in the field (62 B.C.), and his army exterminated. By the suppression of the conspiracy, Cicero earned his title of **Father of his Country**; by his indiscreet use of his power, he brought upon himself exile and loss of influence.

CHAPTER XXIII.

Cæsar, Pompey, and Crassus. — The Gallic Wars.

In the absence of Pompey, the guidance of affairs at Rome had been assumed chiefly by three men, Cato, Cicero, and Cæsar. Crassus, who is sometimes mentioned with them as a leader, was too indolent, and too weak in character, to be of any importance, and was influential only by means of his immense wealth.

Cato was at the head of the senatorial party; Cæsar was the acknowledged chief of the Marians; while Cicero held an intermediate position, depending for his power almost entirely on his unrivalled eloquence, and having the confidence of neither of the two great parties. Of the three, the one whose influence was the greatest was Cæsar. Though bankrupt in fortune, such was the adroitness of his conduct that at every turn of affairs he rose the higher. His star was clearly in the ascendant, when Pompey, after an unwise delay in the East, at length returned to Rome soon after Cæsar had gone to Spain to complete the conquest of Lusitania.

On the return of Pompey, who, during his absence, had become more and more an object of suspicion to the Senate, the city (*cf.* page 96) was comparatively quiet. Cæsar was in Spain; Crassus was unable to form a dangerous opposition; Cato only opposed, with seeming success, the desires of the Eastern Conqueror ; while Cicero was abject in his overtures for friendship.

Cæsar's return from Spain, where he had been entirely successful, offered an opportunity for a change; and every thing was ripe for a coalition against the sena-torial, or ruling, party. **Cæsar, Pompey,** and **Crassus** united their interests, and formed what was called **the first triumvirate.** Cæsar was elected consul. He increased his popularity in every way, — notably, by an agrarian law, so carefully framed and worded that even its enemies could find no fault with it. And, when his term of office was nearly ended, he procured his appointment as proconsul to Gaul for five years, that he might be near Rome, and watch the events at the capital, which his army would enable him largely to control. The Senate more readily agreed to this, as Gaul was at that time in a state of ferment, and threatened serious, if not doubtful, war ; and a failure on the part of Cæsar would remove him from the number of dan-gerous enemies. Cæsar increased his intimacy with Pompey by giving him his daughter Julia in marriage. Before leaving Rome, he procured (58 B.C.) the banish-ment of Cicero, on the ground of putting to death the Catilinian prisoners without a trial; and Cato was sent to Cyprus, to enforce a law by which that island was incorporated in the republic. Cicero was forced to take the proconsulship of Cilicia. It was the design of Cæsar to leave the Senate without a leader who could work injury to his cause during his absence ; and in this he was eminently politic and successful.

News from Gaul now called for his immediate presence (58 B.C.) ; and for nine years he continued his efforts for the subjugation of the country. When peace seemed secure, he even carried his conquests to Britain; and, though he obtained no permanent foothold, he opened the way for the future conquest of the island. During this time, he was called upon to repel several inroads of Germans into Gaul, and pursued them into their own country. It is said that in these wars not less than one million of Gauls and Germans perished. But, if Cæsar made the defeat of his enemies terrible, when war was over, he was a kind and judicious ruler; and by these means he cemented his conquests so firmly to Rome that for centuries the loyalty of Gaul was never shaken; and, even then, not before the empire was tottering with decrepitude, and compelled to leave Gaul to its own devices (52 B.C.).

CHAPTER XXIV.

CÆSAR'S STRUGGLE WITH POMPEY.

DURING the nine years (59–50 B.C.) passed by Cæsar in Gaul, many great events occurred at Rome. In the interior, anarchy prevailed. The republic needed a strong, firm hand, which, at the price even of liberty, should ensure security for it, and stop the shedding of blood. Pompey had attempted to bring about this result; but it was beyond his ability. Shut up at home with his young wife, he let the affairs of state go, and gave up every thing to Clodius, who, since Cicero was exiled, and Cato away from Rome, ruled supreme. Finally, however, Pompey shook off his inertia, and obtained the recall of Cicero (57 B.C.), who returned triumphant, "borne upon the shoulders of all Italy." This was the signal for a reaction against Clodius. Milo placed himself at the head of the Senate, and slew his adversary upon the Appian Way. Pompey, delighted at having got rid of Clodius, obtained the exile of Milo.

During the interval of the two campaigns of 57–56 B.C., Cæsar renewed his alliance with his two colleagues in interviews that took place at Ravenna and Lucca. He renewed for himself the command of Gaul; Pompey, that of Spain; Crassus, that of Syria.

Crassus was jealous of the exploits of Cæsar. He wished also to obtain military renown, and undertook the war against the Parthians. His son, who had distinguished himself in Gaul, accompanied him as lieutenant (55 B.C.). They arrived at Zeugma, a city of Syria, on the Euphrates; and the Romans, seven legions strong, with 4,000 cavalry, drew themselves up along the river. The quæstor Cassius, a man of ability, proposed to Crassus a plan of the campaign, which consisted in following the river as far as Seleucia, in order not to be separated from his fleet and provisions, and to avoid being surrounded by the cavalry of the enemy. But Crassus allowed himself to be deceived by an Arab chief, who allured him to the sandy plains of Mesopotamia.

The forces of the Parthians, divided into many bodies, suddenly rushed upon the Roman ranks, and drove them back. The young Crassus attempted a charge at the head of 1,500 horsemen. The Parthians yielded, but only to draw him into an ambush, where he perished, after great deeds of valor. His head, carried on the end of a pike, was borne before the eyes of his unhappy father, who, crushed by grief and despair, gave the command into the hands of Cassius.

Cassius gave orders for a general retreat. The Parthians subjected the Roman army to continual losses. Crassus, shortly after, was killed (53 B.C.) in a conference.

Thus terminated the expedition of Crassus. In this disastrous campaign there perished more than 20,000 Romans. Ten thousand prisoners were taken, and compelled to serve as slaves in the army of the Parthians.

The death of Crassus broke the triumvirate; that of Julia broke the family ties between Cæsar and Pompey, who then married Cornelia, the widow of the young Crassus.

5*

Cæsar wished to become a second time candidate for the consulship the year following the termination of his proconsulship in Gaul. But he wished first to celebrate his triumph, and would not, on this account, disband his army; for, according to the Roman custom, he could not triumph without it. According to another custom, however, he was obliged to disband it before he could offer himself as a candidate for the consulship. But, setting aside this custom, he demanded permission to become a candidate, while he was in his province in command of the army.

He then intended, after his election, to return with his forces to Rome, celebrate his triumph, and then disband his troops.

The party of Pompey demanded that he should disband his army, come to Rome as a private citizen, and thus sue for the consulship; but he was convinced that such a course could be taken only at the peril of his life.

The question was discussed in the Senate. The party of Pompey was predominant. He had troops in the city; but it was resolved that Cæsar should be ordered to resign his command.

The tribunes opposed the decree, but were not listened to, and were even threatened by the consuls, and compelled to flee. They went directly to Ravenna, on the frontier of Cisalpine Gaul, where Cæsar and his army were stationed.

When Cæsar received the command of the Senate to give up his army, his passion gained the upper hand, and he resolved to march upon Italy. He crossed (49 B.C.) the Rubicon, and went to **Ariminum,** where he met the tribunes who had fled to him.

Here he was met by ambassadors from Pompey, with

orders that he should withdraw from Ariminum, return to Gaul, and disband his army. Cæsar considered this an unjust demand, as it would leave Pompey with entire control over Italy.

Accordingly, he despatched his lieutenant, Marcus Antonius, to take possession of **Arretium**, and himself remained at Ariminum with two legions, and determined to hold a levy there.

He also occupied **Pisaurus**, **Fanus**, and **Ancona**. In a word, all Italy was soon at his feet. Pompey went to Brundisium. He wished to keep this place, in order to have a landing-place for his fleet, in case Cæsar went to Spain.

Cæsar also took this place. He now went to Rome, where he acted as absolute master. He had the treasury broken open, as the keys were concealed; and he disposed of every thing as a sovereign. Thus all Italy was under his control.

In **Spain**, Pompey's party was predominant. **Afranius** and **Petreius**, his lieutenants, were there with seven legions.

Africa was also occupied by his party; and it was confidently hoped that Gaul would rise against Cæsar.

After having arranged matters at Rome, Cæsar marched to Southern Gaul on his way to Spain. He left troops to lay siege to **Massilia**, and hastened himself to Spain.

Afranius and Petreius were stationed at Ilerda, in Northern Spain.

Cæsar brought all his military talent into play, and soon compelled them to capitulate. Thus Cæsar was at once master of all Spain. Shortly afterwards, **Massilia** was also captured.

On his return to Rome, Cæsar was made dictator: within a very short time, he made the most necessary regulations at Rome. After his army had returned from Spain, and new legions were levied, he set out towards Brundisium. It was now nearly twelve months since Pompey had left Rome.

He had taken up his winter quarters in Thessaly, where he had collected troops in great numbers. He also had at his disposal a large fleet.

Cæsar, through the neglect of the Pompeian admirals, crossed the Adriatic unopposed, January, 48 B.C.

With forces very inferior to those of Pompey, Cæsar advanced towards Dyrrachium, and ventured to besiege Pompey, who was stationed there. This was an attack which Pompey did not care much about, as he received his supplies from the sea. Cæsar, who had no such means of providing for his army, was obliged to forage in the country. He tried to bring the war to a close at Dyrrachium. On one occasion, when he made an attack upon the place, he was repulsed with considerable loss. His soldiers began to despond ; and he himself nearly despaired of success.

After this catastrophe, Cæsar left Dyrrachium, and marched through Epirus into Thessaly.

Pompey followed him into Thessaly, where the latter had already chosen his position in the neighborhood of **Pharsalus**, situated upon a rocky eminence, attached to the chain of the Othrys. Pharsalus is surrounded by a vast plain. There was fought one of the decisive battles in the world's history. The army of Pompey, consisting of 47,000 infantry and 7,000 cavalry, was twice as large as that of Cæsar in infantry, and seven times as large in cavalry ; but the disdainful confidence of the Pompeians increased the strength of the well-practised legions of Cæsar.

The battle (August, 48 B.C.) lasted a long time, before either party gained any advantage. Finally, Pompey's forces were defeated. Pompey threw off his insignia of command, mounted his horse, and hastened the shortest way to the sea, and, seeing a vessel weighing anchor, embarked with a few companions, who accompanied him in his flight.

Pompey went to Mitylene, and from there to Egypt, hoping to obtain an asylum from the young king, Ptolemy. Upon his arrival, he was seized and beheaded (28th September, 48 B.C.).

Meanwhile, Cæsar pursued his victory with an indefatigable activity, and set sail for Egypt. Upon his arrival, the head of his enemy was brought to him. Cæsar turned from the sight, with tears in his eyes. The murderers now saw what would be their fate. Ptolemy was at variance with his sister, the famous Cleopatra. Cæsar took the part of the sister against the brother. The inhabitants of Alexandria revolted, and besieged Cæsar in the palace; but, with a handful of soldiers, he bravely baffled their attacks. Setting fire to the neighboring buildings, he escaped to his ships. Afterwards he returned, and wreaked vengeance upon the Alexandrians, establishing Cleopatra firmly upon the throne (47 B.C.).

Satisfied with this vengeance, Cæsar left Egypt and went to Pontus, where Pharnaces, son of Mithridates, was inciting a revolt against Rome.

Cæsar attacked and defeated him at Zela (47 B.C.) with a rapidity rendered proverbial by the words, **Veni, vidi, vici.**

Upon his return to Rome, Cæsar conciliated the people by liberal measures.

Next, Cæsar crossed over into Africa, where the Pompeians gathered around **Cato, Metellus Scipio,** and **Juba,** king of Numidia.

On the 4th of April, 46 B.C., Cæsar invested **Thapsus,** which Scipio endeavored in vain to defend. Scipio wished to take refuge in Spain; but, overtaken by a storm, and fearing to fall into the hands of the enemy, he threw himself into the sea.

Cato took refuge in Utica, and, seeing that all was lost, committed suicide.

The two sons of Pompey, **Cneius** and **Sextus,** fled to Spain, and were the only ones who could now even make a show of resisting Cæsar. After some bloody but indecisive engagements, the Pompeians posted themselves at **Munda** for a final battle. This was fought on the 17th of March, 45 B.C., and ended in a complete victory for Cæsar. Spain submitted.

CHAPTER XXV.

Cæsar Perpetual Dictator. — His Murder.

Cæsar now returned to Rome, and centred in himself all power, creating himself dictator for life, sole consul, tribune, pontifex maximus, &c. The Senate, at the proposal of Cicero, gave him the title of " Father of his Country," and the right to wear a crown of laurels. The fifth month (Quintilis), in which he was born, was named Julius (July).

In his first triumph, he displayed, among other wonders, the Rhine, the Rhone, and the ocean, represented in gold, as a reminder of the conquest of Gaul.

In his second triumph, the images of the Nile, and of Arsinoe, wife of King Ptolemy, were displayed all sparkling in the light.

The third triumph represented Pharnaces and Pontus.

The fourth, Juba, the Moors, and Spain twice subjugated.

Cato, Petreius, and Scipio were represented as piercing themselves with their swords.

Cæsar, now absolute master of Rome and of the entire world, conceived and carried into execution great reforms and useful works. He built a temple to Mars, reformed the calendar, and built a large harbor at Ostia (north of the Tiber); also a road from the Adriatic to the Tyrrhenian sea, over the Apennines.

An immense amphitheatre was built at the foot of the Tarpeian rock in Rome.

In the midst of these plans, he was stopped by death.

Cassius Longinus, an old lieutenant of Crassus, had shown great courage in the war against the Parthians. At Pharsalus, he fought on Pompey's side, but was afterwards pardoned by Cæsar. He was married to a sister of **Brutus,** whom he won over to his designs of a conspiracy for the murder of Cæsar.

Marcus Junius Brutus, nephew and son-in-law of Cato, generous, but narrow-minded, a firm Stoic, had also fought at Pharsalus on Pompey's side, and been pardoned by Cæsar. Cæsar had great affection for him, and called him his son. Brutus believed it his duty to crush all tender sentiments, and to aid Cassius in the re-establishment of the republic.

Cassius, 'twas said, hated the tyrant; and Brutus, tyranny. These conspirators were soon joined by others. Among them were persons of all parties; and men, who had fought against one another at Pharsalus, now went hand in hand. No proposals were made to Cicero, who was at an advanced age, and could not have consented to take away the life of him to whom he himself owed his own. Cæsar's conduct towards those who had fought in the ranks of Pompey, and afterwards returned to him, was extremely noble. All who knew Cicero must have been convinced that he would not have given his consent to the plan of the conspirators. And, if they themselves ever gave the matter a serious thought, they must have owned that it was, in fact, very absurd to fancy that the republic could be restored by the death of Cæsar.

It is said that the murder of Cæsar was the most

senseless act that the Romans ever committed; and a truer word was never spoken.

Cæsar was cautioned in various ways to be on his guard, as more danger threatened him; but to no purpose.

On the morning of the 15th of March, 44 B.C., Decimus Brutus treacherously enticed him to go with him to the Senate-house. As soon as Cæsar took his seat, the conspirators came around him, and Tullius Cimber advanced to pray for the pardon of his exiled brother; and, while the rest joined their entreaties, laid hold of Cæsar's hand, and kissed his head and breast.

As Cæsar resisted their importunity, and suddenly attempted to rise, Cimber, with both hands, pulled Cæsar's garment down from the shoulders; and another, who had placed himself behind the chair, stabbed him in the neck. Turning round, Cæsar seized the dagger, and held it fast. "What are you doing, villain!" he cried. The first blow was struck; and the whole pack fell upon their noble victim. Wherever he turned, he met only bare daggers, and was driven about like a wild beast. Cassius stabbed him in the face, and Marcus Brutus in the groin. He made no more resistance, but wrapped his gown over his head and the lower part of his body, and fell, mortally wounded, at the base of Pompey's statue, which was drenched with blood.

The tumult and commotion were now great; and, in their alarm, most of the senators took to flight. Both parties were blind at the moment, and knew not what was to be done for the future. The tumult at Rome lasted for some days. Cæsar had fallen on the 15th of March, between eleven and twelve o'clock A.M. On

H

the 17th, there was a meeting of the Senate to delibe-
rate upon what was to be done. The conspirators had
fled to the Capitol; and public opinion in the city was
decidedly against them. A great number of Cæsar's
soldiers were in the city, and many others flocked
thither from other parts; and the excitement was so
great that there was ground for apprehending acts of
extreme violence.

At the funeral of Cæsar, Antony, his nearest relative,
delivered the oration. It produced a fearful effect
upon the minds of the people; for he not only dwelt
upon the exploits of Cæsar, amid roars of applause, but,
after he had excited their minds in the highest degree
by his recital, he lifted up the bloody toga, and showed
the people the wounds of the great deceased. The
multitude were seized with such indignation and rage
that, instead of allowing the body to be carried to the
Campus Martius (where it had been resolved to have
it buried), they immediately raised a pile in the
forum, and burnt it there. The people then dispersed
in troops: they broke into the houses of the conspirators, and destroyed them. Brutus and Cassius fled
from the city; and the other conspirators dispersed
over the provinces.

CHAPTER XXVI.

The Second Triumvirate.

Cæsar, in his will, had appointed C. Octavius, the grandson of his sister Julia, heir to three-fourths of his property ; and his other relatives were to have the remaining fourth.

Young Octavius was in his nineteenth year when Cæsar was murdered. When he received the sad intelligence of Cæsar's death, he went to Rome, and claimed the inheritance of his uncle. Cæsar's widow, Calpurnia, had intrusted to Marcus Antonius all the money in the house, — a large sum; and she also had delivered to him all the dictator's writings and memoranda.

The arrival of Octavius to claim his inheritance was disagreeable to Antony; for he was unwilling to let the property go out of his hands, and tried to deter the young man from accepting it.

But Octavius compelled Antony to surrender Cæsar's will ; and he put himself in possession of his inheritance, so far as it had not been already disposed of by Antony, who had secreted a greater part of the money. The exasperation between Octavius and Antony rose very high at this time : each suspected the other of attempts at assassination.

Strengthened by the support of the people and Senate, and by the eloquence of Cicero, who hurled his famous "**Philippics**" against Antony, Octavius appealed to the veterans of Cæsar, and accepted the struggle. Two legions of Antony went over to him. Octavius began a campaign with the two consuls, and seized the camp of Antony, whom he compelled to leave Italy.

Octavius now returned to Rome, was nominated consul, and became reconciled with Antony.

A second **triumvirate** was formed by **Octavius, Antony**, and **Lepidus**, November 27, 43 B.C., forming a self-constituted board of three, who were to rule the state conjointly for **five** years.

The provinces were divided as follows : —

Lepidus was to have Spain and Gallia Narbonensis; Antony, the rest of Gaul beyond the Alps and Gallia Cisalpina ; Octavius, Sicily, Sardinia, and Africa. A bloody proscription followed : among its victims were **Cicero** and 300 senators and 2,000 knights.

The triumvirs could now concentrate their energies upon the East, whither Brutus and Cassius, the murderers of Cæsar, had fled.

In 42 B.C., military operations began. Antony and Octavius crossed from Italy to Epirus, with forces amounting to 130,000 men. They marched unresisted through Epirus and Macedonia, and reached Thrace before they met Brutus and Cassius. These had collected the full strength of the East, amounting to 80,000 infantry and 20,000 cavalry.

The two armies met at **Philippi** (November, 42 B.C.) ; and the fate of the Roman world was decided in a twofold battle.

In the first fight, Brutus defeated Octavius ; but Antony gained a decisive advantage over Cassius, who, unaware of his colleague's victory, committed suicide.

In the second fight, three weeks later, the army of Brutus was completely overcome; and, escaping from the field, he could only follow the example of Cassius, and kill himself.

With Brutus fell the republic. The absolute ascendency of individuals, which is monarchy, was then established.

The immediate result of the victory at Philippi was a fresh arrangement of the Roman world among the triumvirs. As Antony preferred the **East**, Octavius consented to relinquish it to him; and, as a compensation, Italy and Spain were given to Octavius. Africa fell to Lepidus.

Octavius tried to establish order in Italy; but many obstacles were to be overcome. Sextus Pompeius, who had escaped from Munda, by preventing corn-ships from reaching Rome exposed the city to great danger from famine. Octavius was obliged to get together a fleet. At first, he was defeated by Pompey; but finally, in 36 B.C., he conquered him, together with Lepidus, who had joined Pompey through jealousy of Octavius's rising power.

During these events, Antony was in the East, charmed by the fascinations of **Cleopatra**, queen of Egypt. He also began to be jealous of Octavius, who was master of Italy, and at the head of a powerful party. Antony, however, had adopted many customs of the East, and was daily becoming more unpopular at Rome.

Thus, gradually, these two men became more and more estranged, until war was openly declared, and decided at the battle of **Actium**, September 2, 31 B.C. In this battle, Antony cowardly deserted his fleet before the result was decided, and fled with Cleopatra to

Egypt. When Antony fled, his fleet lost heart, and was annihilated. His land force, after waiting a week for his return, surrendered.

Octavius, the next year, went to Egypt; and Antony, after a slight resistance, committed suicide. Cleopatra followed his example.

Octavius was now sole master of the Roman world.

CHAPTER XXVII.

AUGUSTUS.

OCTAVIUS was received with great enthusiasm at Rome; for all were anxious to secure his favor, while they were entirely ignorant as to what course the conqueror would pursue. His first acts, however, removed every fear of a renewal of the proscriptions of Marius and Sulla, and the revival of the dictatorship. While very careful to retain complete control of his conquests, by procuring from the Senate the office of **Imperator**, or general of the armies, he did not hesitate to lay down, of his own free will, all unusual honors which could in any way excite suspicion, and then proceeded to make himself the centre of the state by the vote of the Senate. To restore this body to something of its ancient respectability, he purged it of the additions made by Cæsar and the triumvirate, and put himself at its head as **Princeps**, or chief. It was the policy of the early leaders of the revolution to debase the Senate, the sole relic of the republic, as an enemy, and to destroy it by making it contemptible. It was the policy of Augustus to so far restore its character that, by its authority, he might establish his government on a basis of plausible legality. Under senatorial sanction, he invested himself successively with the consulship, tribunate, censorship, and chief pontificate; while he claimed for himself universal proconsular powers. Thus, while laying down his titles won by the sword, he, in fact, retook them by means of a subservient Senate; and, while pretending to restore the glories of the republic, he deprived it of every republican feature.

The people not only submitted to these usurpations, but encouraged them. Fifty years of civil war had made them anxious for any change which promised peace, and an enjoyment of the vast wealth which was continually pouring in from the provinces. Peace at any price was the universal desire; and it was to this fact that Octavius owed his success.

As the title of king was so obnoxious to the Romans, a new one was invented for Octavius, — that of **Augustus**, which lent him dignity, if it did not increase his authority; and it is by this title that he is generally known. So gradually and unobtrusively were the reforms of Augustus made, and so anxious were the Romans for a rest from strife, that we find only two very harmless attempts to shake his authority; and when he declared the " Roman Peace," closing the gates of the temple of Janus for the first time in more than two hundred years (234 B.C.), the people seem to have been so charmed with their new luxury that they were willing to submit to any rule rather than to endanger it even by a murmur.

One of the first cares of Augustus was to secure the tranquillity of the outlying portions of the empire.

The Parthians in the East, and the Germans on the Rhine, made a protracted struggle against the Roman power, during which the Germans, under Herrman, inflicted on the legions of Varus the most sanguinary defeat which had befallen the Roman arms since the battle of Cannæ. Still, by extending the rights of citizenship to the inhabitants of the provinces, Augustus not only fastened his empire together, but gave to the border nations a new and vital interest in the integrity of its boundaries. By taking the control of provincial affairs into his own hands, he put an end to the misrule of the creatures of the Senate, and replaced tyrannical oppression by firm and even justice. The empire had reached its limits. After Augustus, but two additions, Britain and Dacia, were made to its dominions; and Rome was abundantly satisfied if able to maintain its authority over what it already possessed.

At home, while he remodelled the state, he found time to beautify the capital, and, without burdening his subjects, changed it so completely that he was able to boast that he found the city of brick, and left it of marble.

In his family, the first emperor was singularly unfortunate. Having no sons of his own, he adopted those of his relatives, and saw the most promising of these pass away, and himself threatened with the loss of every heir. The conduct of his only child, Julia, caused her banishment; while his anxiety to prevent the empire from falling to pieces for want of a head did not permit him to disinherit her children.

Augustus died, after seeing his empire well established, at the age of seventy-six years (14 A.D.). He was frugal and correct in his personal habits ; quick and shrewd in his dealings with men ; bold and ambitious in the affairs of state. His greatness consisted rather in the ability to abstain from abusing the advantages presented by fortune than in the genius which moulds the current of affairs to the will. His success depended on the temper of the people and the peculiar circumstances of the time. His clearest title to greatness is found in the fact that he compelled eighty millions of people to live in peace for forty-four years.

In estimating the character of Augustus, we must take into account the writers whose names have given to his its brightest lustre, and have made the **Augustan Age** a synonym for excellence in culture, art, and government. Vergil, Ovid, Horace, Livy, and a host of others, have given his reign a brilliancy unmatched in time, which is rather enhanced than diminished by the fame of Cicero, Cæsar, and Sallust, who preceded him, and Tacitus, Seneca, and others, who came after; for they belong to an epoch in which Augustus stands the central figure in all which pertains to the arts of peace. If Roman art and Roman literature were a copy of the Greek, it was a noble imitation; and if it added to its sublimity, its grace and elegance, a subservience which borders on servility, it is but an evidence of the utter demoralization wrought by the civil wars, and of the ecstasy with which peace filled every mind. Much allowance must be made for the extravagant praises lavished on their hero; and he must be judged by the result of his labors. He made the world to centre on one will; and the destruction of the mighty fabric began the moment it fell to feebler or less sincere hands. The horrors which marked the reigns of his successors were the legitimate result of the irresponsible sovereignty he established. He formed his empire for the present, to the utter ignoring of the future. Thus it would seem, then, that the part he played was that of a shrewd politician, rather than of a wise statesman.

CHAPTER XXVIII.

THE JULIAN EMPERORS.

WE now turn our backs for ever on the old Roman world, the last vestige of which was swept away by Augustus. The virtues, and even the more respectable vices, of the greater Rome, were entire strangers to the empire; and, of all that had made her great, there remained only an empty name and a still emptier pride.

Augustus was succeeded by **Tiberius**, son of Livia, wife of Augustus and her former husband, Tiberius Claudius Nero. During the later years of the life of Augustus, Livia had exercised an almost boundless influence over the emperor, and, as long as she lived, managed to keep her unruly son somewhat within bounds of decency. On the death of Livia, Tiberius confined himself to a retreat at Capreæ, where he abandoned himself to brutal sensuality. His throne was secured by the murder of Agrippa Posthumus, who might, from the popularity of his father's name, have become dangerous; and, somewhat later, by that of Germanicus, his nephew.

Tiberius had shown himself a good soldier and a brave man; and every thing promised well for his reign. But he was morose, sullen, and suspicious. He dared not trust the people, but surrounded himself with a guard of the Prætorians. He dared not trust his son, and set up a favorite, Sejanus, on whom he lavished

every favor, and to whom he intrusted every command. The favorite soon found means to carry off the
young prince by poison, and even looked with longings
to the crown. After a brief rule, the minister fell
under well-merited suspicion, and was put to death.
Then followed a general proscription, in which all
who could interfere with the safety of the state were
sacrificed. Not even yet did Tiberius dare to visit his
capital. Once, indeed, he made the attempt, and sailed
up the Tiber, having guards on either bank, who drove
away the populace gathered to welcome his return.
On coming within sight of the gardens of Cæsar, he
turned back, and did not stop till he regained his island
retreat. Now began a remarkable period of suicides.
The wealthy and wise shrunk from witnessing the
horrors of the times; and many sought to escape by
putting an end to their own lives. The misery of the
reign was, however, confined to the city; and there is
no reason to doubt that the rest of the empire enjoyed
a considerable amount of prosperity. After a reign of
thirteen years (14–27 A.D.), Tiberius died either in a
fainting fit or, as is quite as possible, from being
smothered by his attendants.

CALIGULA (37–41 A.D.).

He was succeeded by **Caius**, son of Germanicus, better known as **Caligula**,— a nickname given him by the
soldiers from the buskins he wore. Caligula was twenty-
five years old when he began to reign. His constitution was weakly. He was subject to fits. He slept
but little, and then was troubled with most frightful
dreams. At first, he showed great moderation and

affability. By burning the accusations sent him by informers, he won the hearts of the people, eager to change the morose old Tiberius for any other master.

This lasted but a very brief time. The celebration of his birthday was on a scale of the greatest grandeur ; and, from that time, he plunged into every excess. An illness caused by these excesses convinced him of the affections of the people ; and, on his recovery, he threw off every restraint. After squandering the wealth he had inherited, he put to death wealthy citizens, and confiscated their possessions. He is said to have expressed a wish that the Roman people had but one neck, that he might slay them all at a blow. His famous bridge, from the Palatine to the capital, was quite equalled by a bridge across the Bay of Baiæ. It may be the intention was to increase the safety of the harbor ; but, at all events, it never served any purpose. During this period of his reign, he found time to make an expedition into Gaul, and even meditated and prepared an invasion of Britain.

After a rule of four years, a conspiracy was formed by a tribune of the Prætorian guard ; and the emperor was assassinated. At first, the Senate endeavored to regain their lost power. But though a strong party was in favor of a return to the republic, so many of the influential citizens put in claims for the vacant office that it became apparent that such a return was now impossible. All doubt was dispelled, however, when the Prætorians discovered Claudius, an uncle of Caligula, hidden in the palace, and, taking him to their camp, proclaimed him emperor (41 A.D.).

CLAUDIUS (41–54 A.D.).

The new monarch had escaped the fate of the other members of the family, only because he did not seem to have wit enough to become dangerous. He, however, appears to have devoted himself to business with much energy and perseverance; and his chief faults, perhaps, were a too great indulgence in the luxuries of the table, and a too ready submission to the rule of his wives. At home, his rule was mild and, without doubt, beneficial. The rigor of his government in the provinces cannot be questioned. The conquest of Britain was undertaken by Claudius; and, after a campaign of but sixteen days, he had laid firmly the foundation of its final subjection.

The last wife of Claudius was his niece, Agrippina, sister to Caligula. This woman had a son by her former husband, Domitius, who was also named **Domitius.** Agrippina induced the emperor to adopt her son, who took the name of **Nero,** by which he is generally known, and, to secure still further his succession, betrothed him to Octavia, daughter of Claudius. Every thing being ripe, the faithless wife caused her husband to be poisoned, and her son to be proclaimed in his stead. Claudius, under the influence of evil counsellors, persecuted some of the noble Romans; but, even in this respect, he was a model of mildness compared with his predecessors. The obloquy which surrounds his name is doubtless due to the necessity of disparaging him, that Nero might be the more favorably received.

NERO (54–68 A.D.).

Nero was sixteen years old when he began (54 A.D.) to reign. During the first five years of his reign, he was under the influence of Seneca and Burrhus, prefect of the Prætorians ; and his government was, with few exceptions, the most respectable since Augustus. It was certainly during this period that Britannicus, son of the late emperor, was put to death. But this was due rather to the fears and policy of Agrippina than to the cruelty or malice of Nero.

His masters kept the young emperor amused, and removed from the cares of state, until he became entangled with Poppæa, wife of Salvius Otho. Both were married ; but Nero, who had only used Octavia as a stepping-stone to fortune, felt no scruples in divorcing her ; and Otho was sent on a distant mission, and afterwards divorced with as little compunction. The only real obstacle was the active and dangerous Agrippina, who was entirely unwilling to share her authority over her son with another. Her death was determined on ; and neither Seneca nor Burrhus felt strong enough to refuse to counsel, or at least connive at, her murder. An attempt was made to drown her in the Bay of Baiæ, and, that failing, she was despatched by the hands of assassins. Poppæa then obtained complete control of the emperor. Octavia was banished, and afterwards murdered, when Poppæa became her successor.

It would be useless to follow the crimes of Nero from this time in detail. Poppæa died from a kick administered by her imperial husband. The wealthy were plundered and put to death. The death of Burrhus

and the withdrawal of Seneca released Nero from every
restraint; and he no longer hesitated to outrage the
feelings of his subjects in every way. He appeared in
public, contending first as a musician and afterwards
in the sports of the circus. The great fire which at
this time destroyed a great part of the city was as-
cribed to him, but without sufficient evidence; and the
stories of his conduct during the conflagration are,
doubtless, pure fictions. It was, however, necessary to
fix the guilt on some one; and the fittest objects appeared to be the Jews and Christians, who were persecuted without mercy, until public opinion compelled
their safety.

Conspiracies now arose, in which Seneca and Lucan
were implicated; and both were ordered to take their
own lives. In a tour made of Greece, Nero conducted
himself so scandalously that even Roman morals were
shocked, and Roman patience could endure him no
longer. The army in hither Spain revolted, and
marched on Rome. Nero felt that he was not safe in
the city, and fled in abject fear to the villa of a freed-
man, Phaon. Here, after a struggle with his horror of
death, which was only overcome by the greater horror
of the punishment decreed against him by the Senate,
he put an end to his own life just in time to escape
capture at the hands of the soldiers. Nero was thirty
years old, and had reigned fourteen years. With him
ended the line of the adopted sons of the Julii.

GALBA (68–69 A.D.).

Galba had been proclaimed emperor by his soldiers,
about two months before the death of Nero; and the

most important features of this revolution were the revolt of the army, and the proclaiming of an emperor elsewhere than at Rome. A precedent was now formed, which was followed many times.

Galba entered the city as a conqueror without much opposition. He soon became unpopular from his parsimony and austerity ; and the selection of Piso Licinianus as an associate did not help matters, as he was too much like Galba in character. The soldiers mutinied ; and the new emperors were murdered the fifteenth day after Galba entered Rome.

OTHO (69 A.D.).

Otho, from whom Nero had taken his wife, Poppæa, was the leader of the insurrection against Galba, and was declared emperor. No sooner did the news of his accession reach Gaul, than Vitellius, a general of the army of the Rhine, revolted. Although safe in Rome, Otho found it necessary to march against the rebels. He was defeated at Bedriacum, near the junction of the Po and Adda, and put an end to his life, after a reign of three months.

VITELLIUS (69 A.D.).

Vitellius became successor to the vacant throne. He was coarse and brutal. His march to Rome was marked by great cruelty and excesses. The Romans were disgusted with him before his arrival. He was therefore compelled to take measures for their conciliation. Thus far, the revolts against the crown had been confined to the West : the East had shown but little in-

6*   I

terest in them.   Now, however, Vespasian, a lieutenant
in Syria, began to attract attention ; and his soldiers
declared him emperor (July 1).   This made the third
imperator who had been declared during the year (69
A.D.).   Unmindful of the threatening dangers, Vitellius, after a few concessions to the people, surrendered
himself to the grossest debauchery ; while Vespasian,
leaving his son Titus to continue the war in Palestine,
took every measure to insure a speedy and successful
march on Rome.   The command of the army was intrusted to Mucianus and Antonius Primus ; and the
war was only concluded in the city itself by the capture
of the Praetorian camp, and the death of Vitellius, who
was murdered with every indignity (December 21,
A.D. 69).

CHAPTER XXIX.

THE FLAVIAN EMPERORS.

VESPASIAN (69–79 A.D.).

VESPASIAN was absent at the Jewish war when he was proclaimed emperor. The Jews had undergone many changes of government since the death of Augustus. They had been separated from the empire, under native princes, and rejoined to it. Under Nero, the oppression of the imperial governors drove the people to a rebellion, which brought to the surface all the fanaticism and frenzy of which human nature is capable. On determining to seize the imperial crown, Vespasian left the conduct of the war to his son Titus, who, as soon as affairs became settled at Rome, marched at once on Jerusalem, and utterly destroyed it. The horrors of the siege were aggravated by every circumstance which can make war terrible. Famine, pestilence, and the sword, discord within the walls, and the unsparing sword of the Romans without, made this one of the most awful of the calamities which stain the pages of history.

The capture of Jerusalem (70 A.D.) virtually ended the war; and Titus hastened to Rome to assist his father. An insurrection in Gaul at one time threatened serious complications; but it disappeared before the first advance of the Roman forces. This rebellion was entirely a military movement; for by this time Gaul had become so thoroughly Romanized that no movement to throw off the imperial yoke was possible among the people.

Vespasian was active and prudent in public affairs, and frugal and virtuous in his private life. His reign of ten years was marked by peace and prosperity at home and abroad.

TITUS (79–81 A.D.).

Vespasian was succeeded by his son Titus, who emulated the virtues of his father to such an extent that he was called the "darling of mankind." His early life had not been exemplary; but, on his accession to the throne, his conduct changed, to the universal delight of his people. His peaceful reign has left its monuments in the ruins of the Colosseum (which had been begun by his father), the arch, and baths of Titus at Rome. It was during this reign that the cities of Herculaneum and Pompeii were destroyed by an eruption of Vesuvius, being covered and preserved as an example of the civilization and culture of the empire at the period of its highest grandeur.

After a prosperous and happy reign of two years, Titus left his throne to his brother Domitian, who has been suspected of having carried off his brother by poison. This suspicion, however, is due to the subsequent career of Domitian, rather than to any evidence of his guilt.

DOMITIAN (81–96 A.D.).

Domitian departed entirely from the virtue and simplicity of his predecessors. While indulging in every luxury, he endeavored to reform the state. To support his extravagances, and the demands of the army, he levied forced loans on the people, — a sure sign of weakness and misgovernment. He lived in constant dread of assassination, and oppressed and irritated all classes, especially the nobles. He was murdered, after a reign of fifteen years, during which he earned the hatred and contempt of his subjects by his crimes and inconsistencies. With Domitian, ended the line of **Flavian emperors.** He was also the last of those known as the **Twelve Cæsars.**

Nerva (96–98 a.d.).

Domitian was succeeded by Cocceius Nerva, who was appointed by the Senate, and was the first emperor who did not owe his advancement to military force or influence. Nerva associated with himself M. Ulpius Trajan, then in command of the army on the Rhine. Nerva survived his elevation but sixteen months ; but during that time he had curbed the Prætorian guard, whose camp within the city gave them an almost supreme influence over the government, restored tranquillity to the people, and avoided giving offence to any, while conferring happiness and prosperity on every class.

Trajan (98–117 a.d.).

Nerva was succeeded by Trajan, without a murmur on the part of the people. The character of Trajan has its surest guarantee in the love and veneration of his subjects ; and it is said that, long afterwards, the highest praise which could be bestowed on a ruler was that he was "more fortunate than Augustus, and better than Trajan." Trajan was a soldier ; and, if he lacked the refinements of peaceful life, he was nevertheless a wise and firm master.

He added to the empire Dacia, the country included between the Danube and the Theiss, the Carpathians and the Pruth. This territory became so thoroughly Romanized that the language of its inhabitants to-day is founded on that of their conquerors of nearly eighteen centuries ago. It was in honor of his campaign into Dacia that Trajan erected his famous column at Rome, which still remains.

After the Dacian war, Trajan remained a few years at Rome, where he expended vast sums in public improvements ; but the money so expended was the fruit of his wars, not spoils forced from his subjects. The last two years of his reign were spent in wars against the Parthians and Armenians. In these he was so successful as to add them to the empire ; but the bond which held them was so loose that they fell away immediately on his death. Trajan died after a reign of nineteen years, during which he enjoyed almost uninterrupted prosperity.

There had been a great change in the feelings of the Roman people since we saw them opposing so strongly the admission of the Italians to citizenship, as may be seen from the fact that Trajan was not only not a Roman citizen, but was not even born in Italy. The family from which he descended had been for a long time settled in Spain, whither they had immigrated from the imperial city.

HADRIAN (117–138 A.D.).

Trajan was succeeded by P. Ælius Hadrianus, son of his cousin, and also a native of Spain. One of the first acts of Hadrian was to relinquish the recent conquests of Trajan, and to restore the old boundaries of the empire. The reasons of this are obvious. The utmost limits had already been reached which could lend strength to the power of Rome, or be held in subjection without constant and expensive military operations. The people occupying the new conquests were hardy and warlike, scattered through a country easy of defence, and certain to strive continually against a foreign yoke.

The early portion of the reign of Hadrian was full of labor and hardship. He was constantly busied in different parts of the empire struggling to preserve the boundaries which had been established before Trajan, and in repressing rebellion. He was scarcely on the throne before disturbances arose everywhere. He visited Britain, where he curbed the inroads of the Caledonians, and built a fortified line of works (known as the Picts' Wall), extending from sea to sea. He made an expedition into Dacia, but found it useless to attempt to hold the country. Thence he was called in haste to Rome to quell an insurrection, which he accomplished with merited severity. He was compelled to visit the East, where the Jews were making serious trouble by a revolt, and completed their dispersion by their overthrow. Indeed, there was scarcely a portion of his vast domain which did not seem to demand his presence, and to which he did not journey.

On his return to Rome, Hadrian devoted himself to the adornment of the city. Several of his works, more or less complete, as his Mole, or tomb, still remain to us.

Hadrian was afflicted with poor health, suffering much by diseases from which he could find no relief.

To secure a proper succession, he associated with himself in the government Titus Aurelius Antoninus, and required him to adopt M. Annius Verus, his sister's son, and Lucius Verus, a child. Soon after this arrangement was made, Hadrian died (138 A.D.), and left the empire to Titus and his sons.

CHAPTER XXX.

The Antonines (138–192 A.D.).

Antoninus Pius (138–161 A.D.).

Of the new emperors, Antoninus was already fifty-two years old. He was a native of Gaul, and well earned the name by which he is universally known, "Pius." This title was conferred upon him by the Senate as a mark of affectionate respect which he had showed for Hadrian. Aurelius was much younger, — not yet twenty years old, — and was connected with his colleague by marriage with his daughter, Faustina.

The Antonines ruled solely with a view to making their people happy; and, with the exception of Augustus, none of the emperors are so distinguished. Frugal almost to parsimony in what concerned themselves, they were lavish in their expenditures for the benefit of the state. By wisdom and prudence, they succeeded in winning the respect and affection both of the soldiers and nobles, and caused the affairs of state to move so smoothly that their reign presents but few of the incidents of which history is made. On their accession, conspiracies were formed against them; but these were easily quelled, and the twenty-four years of their reign are years of honorable and dignified tranquillity.

Marcus Aurelius (161–180 A.D.).

On the death of Antoninus, Marcus associated with himself Verus, of whom Antoninus had taken no notice

during his reign. The troubles of Marcus began with
his accession. The Moors had made an irruption into
Spain ; barbarians had broken into Gaul ; the army in
Britain had attempted to set up Statius Priscus as emperor ; and the attitude of Parthia in the East was
threatening. The eastern war was fortunately terminated ; but the returning army brought with it a pestilence, which spread devastation throughout the West.
An insurrection on the Danube called for the greatest
activity on the part of the empire, and was only partially settled.

The early death of Verus (168 A.D.) released Marcus
from a colleague who attracted attention only by his
unfitness for his position, and relieved the emperor of
embarrassments which might well have become his
greatest danger.

The remainder of his reign, however, was scarcely
less unhappy. One of his generals revolted in the East,
but was put to death by his own soldiers. Scarcely
had Marcus returned to Rome, when he was called
against the Sarmatians. Rome had now not only
passed the age of conquest, but had outlived her ability
to defend what she already possessed. Marcus died
(180 A.D.) before peace was made with these barbarians,
— a peace which was purchased from them with money,
by his thus setting the example, so often followed in
later times, of buying with gold what Rome lacked
strength and courage to enforce by arms.

Marcus Aurelius was the " Philosopher " of the empire. His tastes were quiet; he was unassuming, and
honestly intent on the good of his people. Their wel-
fare drove him into active military life, full of cares
and hardships from which he never shrank. His faults

were amiable weaknesses; his virtues, those of a hero. With him ended the line of "good emperors."

COMMODUS (180–192 A.D.).

Commodus, who succeeded Marcus, was the unworthy son of an indulgent father. His mother was Faustina, daughter of Antoninus, a lady whose name has become even more dishonorable than she deserved on account of the vices of her son.

On the death of Marcus, Commodus hastened to Rome, and was received by both the Senate and army without opposition. His character, tolerably well veiled before his accession, soon became apparent. He united the low tastes of the gladiator with a ferocity and vindictiveness almost unequalled even among the emperors of unhappy Rome. His sister conspired against his life; but the assassin was unsuccessful. As he struck the blow, he said, "The Senate sends you this;" and from that moment Commodus persecuted the Senate with unrelenting hate. Informers were highly rewarded; and by their means he rid himself of the most distinguished members of that body. He gave the government into the hands of ministers so ingenious in their corruption, that even the patient Roman populace rose against them, and demanded their lives. Commodus abandoned his favorites without compunction. Owing to misrule, the army in Britain joined in the demand for their punishment; and they paid the penalty of their crimes with their lives.

At length, a conspiracy of his servants rid the empire of this monster, after a reign of twelve years. He was the equal of Nero in his crimes, the inferior in every manly attribute except brute strength; a monarch whose proudest boasts were his triumphs in the amphitheatre, and his ability to kill a hundred lions with a hundred arrows.

CHAPTER XXXI.

PERIOD OF MILITARY DESPOTISM (193–306 A.D.).

PERTINAX (192–193 A.D.).

COMMODUS was succeeded by Pertinax, the prefect of the city, an old and distinguished senator (192 A.D.). Pertinax was a well-meaning, conscientious statesman, and did what he could to restore tranquillity to the city. He corrected abuses, and recalled many citizens who had been banished under Commodus. It was his misfortune to have no military support with which to enforce his measures, and provide for his own safety. After a reign of three months, the Prætorian guard broke into revolt, and ended his reforms by his murder.

JULIANUS (193 A.D.).

The Prætorians then set the imperial crown up at auction, and sold it to the highest bidder. The man who sought to purchase the debased honors of his country was Didius Julianus. He enjoyed them but two months, when he was deposed, condemned, and executed.

SEPTIMUS SEVERUS (193–211 A.D.).

In the mean time, several soldiers had been declared emperor by their respective armies. Among these was Septimus Severus, an African, belonging to the army of the Danube. Severus at once marched on Rome;

and, at his approach, the Prætorians deserted their creature for the new master, making for themselves the best terms they could. They were disarmed, and banished from the city. Secure of the capital, Severus devoted himself to subduing the other aspirants for the purple, which occupied his attention for three years. Returning to Rome, he put out of the way all of the senators who were unfriendly to him, and, having thus insured the stability of his rule, spent most of his time abroad. He died in Britain, where he carried on a considerable war against the barbarians of the North, after a reign of eighteen years (211 A.D.).

CARACALLA (211–217 A.D.).

Severus left two sons, both of whom he had associated with himself in the government. No sooner was he dead than they quarrelled with each other; and the elder, Bassianus, better known by his nickname of Caracalla, murdered his brother with his own hands.

Caracalla was one of the most bloody-minded of the Roman emperors; and his name is linked by his crimes to those of Nero and Commodus. There was nothing in his character to admire or respect. The number of his illustrious victims is said to have amounted to several thousands. He spent most of his time away from Rome, everywhere displaying the same wanton cruelty. After a reign of six years, he was murdered by a common soldier (217 A.D.).

MACRINUS (217–218 A.D.).

Caracalla was succeeded by Macrinus, who perished the next year in an attempt to reduce the pay of the soldiers. The military were the power behind the throne. They made and unmade the monarchs, as we have seen. That their pay was too large is certain; for it was the price of their toleration of a master. But they were all-powerful; and any attempt to curtail their privileges was full of danger.

HELIOGABALUS (218–222 A.D.).

Heliogabalus, a priest of the sun, at Edessa, was next raised to the throne. This man had few virtues; but his vices seem to have been entirely of a personal character. He, however, carried these to such an extent as to disgust all his subjects. After a reign of three years, the Prætorians revolted, and murdered him (222 A.D.).

ALEXANDER SEVERUS (222–235 A.D).

Heliogabalus had associated with himself Alexander, who took the name of Severus, a youth, seventeen years of age; and by him he was succeeded. Alexander proved one of the mildest and most virtuous of the Roman emperors. For a time, he was greatly influenced by his mother, a crafty woman, of much talent, at whose instigation some cruelties were perpetrated. The Prætorians soon perceived that the young emperor proposed to be master, and rebelled. Not, indeed, against Alexander, but against his minister, Ulpian, one of the most distinguished of Roman jurists. Alexander, supported by the people, in vain endeavored to save Ulpian, whom they put to death; and the emperor was for a time compelled to dissemble before his soldiers.   Afterwards, however, the crime was punished.

Alexander's reign was, at first, free from wars; so he was enabled to devote himself to the advancement of his subjects.   He curbed the soldiers, and protected the people, releasing them from many taxes, and secured for them unusual tranquillity and prosperity.   In the latter portion of his reign, he undertook a war against Persia, which resulted in the loss of a portion of Mesopotamia.   Thence he was called to the Danube to resist the Sarmatians and Germans, when he was soon after murdered by his soldiers, under the lead of a gigantic peasant, a Thracian, named Maximinus, after a reign of thirteen years (235 A.D.).

For some time, the history of Rome becomes quite barren.   The names of her rulers have nothing of interest connected with them.   The state drifted along, monarch after monarch rising and falling in rapid succession, and leaving nothing but a name to tell that he had lived.

In the mean time, her enemies on the frontiers were becoming daily more dangerous and threatening.   In the West, the movement of the German tribes had begun, which ended in the conquests of Gaul and Britain. On the Danube, the Goths had made their appearance, and were soon found scouring both land and sea, and carrying off their plunder to their wild homes in the North.   In the East, Persia had just undergone a revolution which had placed a native dynasty on the throne ; and was now able to regain its power and dignity, and to maintain an advantageous war against Rome, lasting many years.

MAXIMINUS (235–238 A.D.).

The usurpation of Maximinus was strongly resented by the Senate, though it was as yet powerless to offer open resistance. Gordian, prefect of Africa, and his son, were, however, encouraged to assume the purple. They met with reverses in the field : the son was killed, and the father put an end to his own life. In encouraging the Gordians, the Senate had taken a step from which there was no retreat. On hearing of their misfortune, it at once placed Maximus and Balbinus on the throne in opposition to Maximinus, and, at the urgent demand of the people, added to them, as " Cæsar," a third Gordian. The end came speedily. Maximinus was murdered by his guards (238 A.D.) ; and, about five months later, Maximus and Balbinus suffered the same fate at the hands of the Prætorians.

THE GORDIANS (238–244 A.D.).

The Gordians (I., II., and III.) were now sole emperors, and put the management of the government into the hands of their minister, Misitheus, who corrected considerably the manners of the court. In 242 A.D., Gordian III. opened the gates of the temple of Janus for the last time in history, and marched in person against the Persians, over whom he gained a brilliant victory. He was soon after murdered by his soldiers, at the instigation of Philippus, an Arabian (244 A.D.), by whom he was succeeded.

PHILIP (244–249 A.D.).

The five years of this reign present nothing of interest, unless it be the fact that Philip has been claimed

7   J

as a convert to Christianity, on no sufficient grounds. His army in Mæsia revolted; and Decius, the officer sent to suppress the rebellion, after defeating the pretender, placed himself at the head of the soldiers, and assumed the purple. Philip met them at Verona, where he was defeated and slain (249 A.D.).

DECIUS (249–251 A.D.).

Decius undertook the rôle of a reformer. He was of old Roman stock, and earnestly sought the restoration of the early traditions. He was soon called to march against the Goths, by whom he was twice defeated, and finally slain. Decius was the first Roman emperor who fell on the field of battle (251 A.D.).

GALLUS (251–253 A.D.).

The Senate at once appointed Gallus to the vacant throne, who obtained from the Goths a momentary peace for a considerable payment in money. The purchase raised a cloud of enemies against Gallus at Rome, and induced the Goths speedily to renew their assault on the empire. Æmilianus, an officer of the army of the Danube, headed a revolt. The emperor was assassinated; and Æmilianus was raised by the soldiers to the throne thus made vacant (253 A.D.).

ÆMILIANUS (253 A.D.).

Æmilianus was not without a claim on the gratitude of the people. He had boldly attacked the Goths on their last inroad, and driven them beyond the Danube. He was, however, allowed no time to demonstrate his fitness or unfitness for rule. Valerian quickly brought against him a powerful army from Gaul and Germany; and, deserted by his own troops, Æmilianus fell, like his predecessor, by the hand of an assassin, after a reign of but three months.

VALERIAN (253–259 A.D.).

Valerianus associated with himself Gallienus; and a poorer choice could scarcely have been made. The Franks had become very troublesome in Gaul; and against them Gallienus pretended to march. He, however, remained at Treves, leaving the conduct of the campaign to a general. The empire was now sorely beset. The Franks carried their depredations through Spain, and even crossed to Africa. The Alemanni (Germans) appeared before Ravenna; and the emperor was fain to purchase peace by marrying Pipa, the daughter of their king. The Goths were even more open and bold in their ravages than before. Sapor, king of Persia, attacked the empire on the East; and Valerian hastened to oppose him. The Persians were victorious near Edessa (259 A.D.); and Valerian was captured. Sapor is said to have used his prisoner with every indignity, compelling Valerian to assist him in mounting his horse, and to perform other degrading offices, and, after his death, to have had his skin stuffed and hung in a temple. It is to these misfortunes that Valerian owes his greatest fame.

GALLIENUS (259–268 A.D.).

No effort was made by Gallienus to repair the for-
tunes of Rome in the East; and the Persians would
have continued in their victorious career, but for the
bravery of Odenathus, king of Palmyra, who took the
title of Augustus, and defended effectually his own
territory from the Persians.

In every part of the empire now arose claimants to
imperial honors, who generally looked to the complete
sovereignty of the empire, with occasionally one more
modest than his fellows, whose ambition did not extend
beyond his own frontier. Of the latter class was Odenathus, who was the only one on whom Gallienus called
for assistance, and on whom the title was legitimately
bestowed. These usurpers are known as the **Thirty
Tyrants,** although their number was but nineteen or
twenty. After an inaction of about six years, Gallienus marched to the Italian frontier against one of
these aspirants (Aureolus), and was killed in a tumult
in his own camp (268 A.D.).

CLAUDIUS (268–270 A.D.).

The final act of Gallienus was the nomination of
Claudius as his successor, — a man who was able to restore for a moment a share of success to the arms of
Rome, and some dignity to her name. He gained a signal
victory over the Goths, who had invaded the empire
in large numbers, and destroyed their fleet. So great
was the disaster that almost the entire body perished
before the end of the next year. In honor of this vic-

tory, Claudius added the title of " Gothicus " to his name. He also concluded a treaty with the rest of the Goths and the Vandals, and received the Gætæ, another barbarous tribe, into friendship. He increased the efficacy of the army by salutary reforms; but was cut off by pestilence, after a brilliant reign of two years.

AURELIAN (270–275 A.D.).

Claudius's successor was an Illyrian peasant, named Aurelian, who proved himself one of the ablest generals of the imperial line. Aurelian defeated the Goths, but recognized the necessity of abandoning the northern bank of the Danube. He also defeated · the Alemanni; but, being called elsewhere, left two of his generals to complete their destruction. The barbarians broke through the Roman lines; and it was only after three bloody battles (at Placentia, Pisa, and Pavia) that they were finally overthrown.

Having restored peace in the West, he marched against Zenobia, queen of Palmyra, who had succeeded to that kingdom on the death of her husband, Odenathus. In this lady Aurelian found a worthy foe, one whose political ability was rendered more brilliant by her justice and courage. Defeated in the field, she fortified herself in Palmyra, which was taken after a siege, and, having rebelled, was destroyed. Zenobia was taken to Rome, where she graced the triumph of Aurelian, and was permitted to live in a private station.

Aurelian was the first who built the walls of Rome in their present position. They have since been several times rebuilt, but on the same lines. He was engaged in an expedition against Persia, when he was murdered

(275 A.D.) by one of his generals. So salutary was the influence of the last two reigns that the empire was without a master for six months ; and yet there arose neither rebellion nor usurper. At length, the army requested the Senate to appoint a successor ; and Tacitus was chosen.

TACITUS (275–276 A.D.).

Tacitus was over seventy years old when he began to reign ; and five months of exertion were all his wasted strength permitted. He died in an expedition against the Alani.

PROBUS (276–282 A.D.).

The army now selected Probus, an Illyrian, and an excellent general, as their chief, who for six years more than sustained the now fast-fading honors of the Roman arms. He defeated and drove back into Germany a most formidable conjunction of barbarians, inflicting on them so severe a blow that one of their principal tribes was never heard of afterwards. He compelled an honorable peace from Persia; and, after suppressing several revolts, finally fell by the hand of an assassin (282 A.D.), because the soldiers were no longer willing to submit to the discipline necessary to make them useful.

CARUS (282–283 A.D.).

Carus, a native of Gaul, was appointed next emperor by the soldiers. Carus was sixty years of age, but vigorous enough to signalize his accession by the defeat of the Sarmatians. He then marched to the East, leaving his son, Carinus, in charge of the western portion of the empire, and taking Numerian, another son, with him. He led his forces further than the emperors had previously penetrated beyond the Tigris ; but there his career was cut short by the dagger of Aper, one of his generals, or, as has been reported with much less probability, by a stroke of lightning (A.D. 283). Numerian led back the forces of his father to a place of safety. In less than two years, both the sons of Carus had fallen ; and Diocles, or Diocletianus, had been placed in their stead.

DIOCLETIAN (284–305 A.D.).

Diocletian was a native of Dalmatia. He had been elected before the death of Carinus, after which he mounted the throne, a successful usurper, as sole and undisputed monarch of the Roman world. Seeing the necessity for a more united country and a firmer rule, Diocletian associated with himself, in the second year of his reign, Maximian, a gigantic soldier, who signalized his accession by subduing a dangerous revolt of the peasantry in Gaul.

The empire had long been constantly, though slowly, disintegrating; and the bonds which held it together were now very feeble. The war with Persia had become chronic ; the Goths threatened the frontier on the Danube, the Germans that on the West ; Britain revolted under Carausius, and Africa under Julian ; the peasants of Gaul rose to relieve themselves of the double burden of spoliation by the enemy and taxation by the government. From this, we can appreciate the state of affairs which induced Diocletian to associate, as Cæsars, Galerius and Constantius (A.D. 292), the former of whom was given charge of the East, and finally compelled an honorable peace from Persia, soon to be broken, however; while the latter restored order to the West. The war in Africa occurred later; but the causes which made it possible were fully recognized.

Having united the empire by multiplying its rulers, all of whom worked in harmony, Diocletian introduced other sweeping changes into the state. Old Rome was dead. Her Senate had lost the last remnant of its respectability. Her censors, tribunes, — all the signs and tokens of her freedom, — were gone; and their last vestige was now swept away. The crown and a court were adopted by each emperor, who no longer even pretended to regard Rome as the capital. The government was consolidated by centring every office in the crown; and the nominally limited monarchy became unreservedly dependent on the will of its master. The seat of government was changed according to the necessities of the times or the caprice of the rulers. Rome was deserted by the court; and Milan, Nicomedia, or any other place which struck the fancy, or offered inducements to the emperor, became for the moment her successor. Now each emperor had his court and his capital; and Rome, except in her traditions, was but little more than a provincial town.

The new arrangement worked miracles. As Galerius had succeeded in the East, and Constantius in Britain, so Diocletian put an end to a serious revolt in Africa, and Maximian drove the Germans beyond the frontier. Having imposed peace and good order on the world, Diocletian and Maximian surprised their subjects by resigning the purple, and withdrawing to private life (305 A.D.).

Instead of allowing the two Cæsars to assume the rank of Augusti, and to nominate each a Cæsar to assist himself, Diocletian placed this very important matter in the hands of his son-in-law, Galerius. The choice for the East fell on an Illyrian shepherd, who assumed the name of Maximinus; and for the West (passing over the claims of Constantine, son of Constantius), on Flavius Severus.

THE SIX EMPERORS OF ROME (306–323 A.D.).

Constantius died at York, Britain, the year after the abdication; and the army of Britain declared Constantine, his son, to be his successor. Except in the extreme West, however, the empire was ruled by Galerius and Severus, as Augusti, or emperors, who recognized Constantine only as Cæsar. Rome now seized an opportunity to regain her prominence, and, as the emperors had chosen Nicomedia and Milan for their capitals, looked about for some one to oppose against them. The Romans were further urged to this by an attempt to levy taxes on them; for, since the conquest of Macedon, citizens of Rome had been exempt from personal taxation.

Choice fell upon Maxentius, who, as the son of Maximian, and, as he had married a daughter of Galerius, promised to meet with but little opposition. Maxentius was a weak, vicious prince; but his father still lived to assist him. Severus marched to dethrone him; and, at the request of both the Senate and the people, Maximian resumed the purple. Severus was overcome, and put to death (307 A.D.); and, to strengthen the cause of his son, Maximian visited

7*

Constantine, heaping upon him every honor, and giving him his daughter in marriage. Constantine wisely refused to commit himself to either party.

An invasion of Italy by Salerius was repelled; and, seeing no way to impair the power of the new emperor of the West but by multiplying the office, he created Licinius emperor, and at the same time was compelled to recognize the right of Maximin, who had usurped the power in Egypt and Syria, to the same rank and title. Thus the Roman world was now in the hands of six emperors (308 A.D.), — Maximian, Maxentius, and Constantine in the West, and Galerius, Licinius, and Maximin in the East.

This state of affairs could not continue. Maximian and his son quarrelled about the possession of Italy before affairs were fairly settled. The father escaped to Constantine, who was compelled to put him to death to prevent his seizing the entire West (310 A.D.). The next year, Galerius died from disease. Maxentius now attempted to come into collision with Constantine, and, failing to provoke that cautious ruler to action, raised an immense army to invade Gaul. His trouble was that any tax which he could collect in Italy was insufficient to maintain him in the reckless extravagance of his career.

Constantine moved at once on Italy; and, after a series of brilliant victories, defeated Maxentius at Saxa Rubra, near Rome, who was drowned in attempting to escape from the field (312 A.D.). The family of the deceased emperor were all put to death by his brother-in-law; but no general massacre was allowed. Licinius and Constantine appeared to be firm friends; and Licinius married the sister of the western monarch, which might be supposed to cement their union. Licinius soon overcame Maximin (313 A.D.) ; and thus the six emperors of Rome dwindled away to two.

Licinius abused his power by putting to death the children of Maximin; but he affixed an indelible stain on his name, and forfeited every claim to sympathy in his own distress, by his persecutions of the wife and daughter of Diocletian. After driving them from place to place, he ordered them put to death.

The peace between the East and the West lasted about a year, when a quarrel arose which enabled Constantine to add Macedonia and Greece to his possessions. For about nine years nothing occurred to disturb the serenity of their relations ; and both seemed satisfied with the existing state of affairs. Constantine then invaded the East without provocation (323 A.D.), defeated Licinius in two pitched battles, and once more united the government of the world in his own person. Licinius was soon after put to death, though he had surrendered all his honors to the conqueror (324 A.D.).

CHAPTER XXXII.

Constantine the Great (306–327 A.D.).

Having attained the undivided sovereignty, Constantine determined to build for his empire a new capital, which should be worthy of him. He selected the site •of **Byzantium** as offering the greatest advantages; for, being defended on two sides by the sea and the Golden Horn, it could easily be made almost impregnable, while as a seaport its advantages were unrivalled, — a feature not in the least shared by Rome. The project was entered upon with characteristic energy; and the city was built. To people it, the seat of government was permanently removed thither; and every inducement was offered to immigration. The empire was now , repartitioned and reorganized. Thus was born the Greek empire, destined to drag out a miserable existence for nearly a thousand years after Rome had fallen a prey to the barbarians.

The later years of his reign did not add much to the fame of Constantine. He became jealous of his own family, and hired informers to testify against them. Among the more illustrious of his victims were his son Crispus, who had shown himself in every way worthy to become his successor, and the empress, Fausta, daughter of Maximian. A bright spot in his declining years was the defeat of the Goths. These invaded the empire, but were repelled with all the vigor and energy which characterized his youth. Constantine died, after a reign of thirty years, in the sixty-fourth year of his age (337 A.D.).

Constantine earned his title of "Great" by his military talents, his bravery, and his wisdom. He is entitled to great credit for the uniform kindness with which he treated his Christian subjects. It is said that his mother, Helena, was a Christian, and that it was to her influence that this mildness was due. Very early in the existence of the empire the struggle between the religion of Christ and that of Rome had attracted attention. A compromise was usually made by the Romans after a conquest, by their adopting the gods of the vanquished into their own mythology, and introducing their own gods into that of their new subjects. In the case of the Christians, no such arrangement was possible. Under several of the emperors, they suffered severe persecution ; and all calamities were unhesitatingly laid at their doors. Even Diocletian, at the instigation of Galerius, did not scruple to decree most violent measures against them, but with no more permanent result than had followed similar action on the part of his predecessors. The sect had increased, and in the main had prospered, until now, under Constantine, we find them very powerful in the state ; and after him the old religion was swept away beyond the possibility of revival. Thus, whether the favor of Constantine was due to early training, or to the recognition of the certainty of the ultimate predominance of Christianity and a desire to gain the support of an already powerful faction, the fact remains that, under him, the Christians became the dominant body, and their advancement did infinite credit to either his head or his heart.

The great deeds of Constantine were the uniting of the Roman world; the change of capital, resulting in the final separation of the East from the West; and the establishment of Christianity as the religion of the state. In person, he was tall and majestic; he was dexterous in all warlike accomplishments; he was intrepid in war, affable in peace; he was patient and prudent in council, bold and unhesitating in action. He was prudent in adversity; but he did not seem able to bear prosperity. Ambition alone led him to attack the East; and the very madness of jealousy marked his course after his success. He was filial in his affection toward his mother; but he can scarcely be called affectionate who put to death his father-in-law, his brother-in-law, his wife, and his son. If he was great in his virtues, in his faults he was contemptible.

CONSTANTINE II., CONSTANTIUS, CONSTANS (337–353 A.D.).

Constantine was succeeded by his three sons, Constantine, Constantius, and Constans, who divided the empire among themselves. Constantius and Constans almost immediately went to war over the possession of Italy, which belonged by right to Constans. The difficulty ended in the death of Constantine; and for some time the two remaining brothers lived in harmony, because the Persian war in the East occupied the one, while the other was satisfied with a life of indolence and dissipation. Constans was murdered by his soldiers (350 A.D.); and Constantius had little difficulty in uniting the empire. The eastern war was prosecuted with some vigor, until at length it became apparent that nothing could be gained by it ; and then peace was concluded.

While Constantius was thus engaged, his nephew, Julian, was winning for himself laurels in the West by his energetic and successful movements against the Germans. In these he was so fortunate that he excited the jealousy of the emperor, who ordered him to Constantinople. The troops mutinied on receipt of the order, and compelled Julian to assume the purple, and to march to the East. Constantius hastened to meet him ; but, worn out by his cares and labors, he died on the way (360 A.D.), and was quietly succeeded by his rival.

JULIAN (360–363 A.D.).

Julian was a good soldier, and was a man calculated to win the love and respect of all. He had been educated a Christian, but had been won over by the philosophers of the day, and attempted to restore the old religion ; thus gaining for himself the epithet of " Apostate." The change made by Constantine had given to the Christians too firm a hold in the state to admit of their power being shaken ; and the failure of Julian precluded for ever afterward any attempt at such a revolution.

Julian was scarcely more successful in an invasion which he made into Persia. Deceived by his guides, he pushed far into the country ; the Persian monarch refusing an engagement, and retiring before him. When it became necessary to retreat, the rear of the Romans was attacked, and was saved only by the courage and management of Julian. He was mortally wounded in a surprise (363 A.D.).

JOVIAN (363–364 A.D.).

Jovian was selected on the field as the successor of Julian. He led the army into safety, but died before reaching Constantinople, after a reign of seven months.

VALENTINIAN AND VALENS (364–375 A.D.).

After a brief interregnum, the throne was bestowed on Valentinian, who associated with himself his brother Valens; and the empire was divided for a third time, and this time finally. Valens received for his share the East, with Constantinople as his capital. Valentinian took the West, making Milan the seat of his government. So completely had Rome fallen from her ancient position, that it is very doubtful if Valentinian visited the city during the twelve years of his reign. His time was chiefly occupied in repelling invasions of the barbarians into Gaul; and he died during a campaign on the Danube (375 A.D.). Although he was able for the time to repulse his enemies, he could not produce any permanent effect.

GRATIAN (375–383 A.D.).

Valentinian was succeeded by his eldest son, Gratian, who followed the footsteps of his father in discouraging Paganism, and increasing the spread of Christianity. He adopted his half-brother, Valentinian, and conferred upon him every honor. The reign of Gratian was quite prosperous as regarded the frontiers, and was peaceful at home. It was at this time that Valens was slain in battle against the Goths; but so completely were the two empires sundered, that Gratian, instead of attempting to bring them under one rule, appointed Theodosius to the vacant throne.   –

Gratian now gave himself up to pleasure, under the direction of Alaric, a barbarian. His soldiers in Britain became dissatisfied, and mutinied under a leader named Maximus.

MAXIMUS (383–388 A.D.).

Gratian hastened to oppose the usurper; but his troops refused to fight, and he was compelled to seek aid from Valentinian II. He was captured and put to death, while on his journey (383 A.D.).

VALENTINIAN II. (387–392 A.D.).

Valentinian appealed to the eastern emperor; but the only assistance he could obtain was a guarantee that Maximus should not interfere with Italy, Illyrium, and Africa. These stipulations were observed for about four years, when Maximus suddenly appeared before Milan, which Valentinian had made his capital; and he, and his mother, who was regent during his minority, had barely time to escape. Theodosius now moved, and arrayed an army of Huns, Goths, and other barbarians, against the Germans and Gauls, who supported Maximus; while the Romans looked on, without, apparently, taking much interest in the result. Maximus was overthrown and slain (388 A.D.). For three years, Theodosius remained in Italy, wielding the real power in both empires, while he permitted Valentinian to re-install himself in his imperial office. Shortly after his departure, Valentinian was assassinated by a general of the Franks (392 A.D.), who, however, declined to seize the throne, but placed on it Eugenius, a man of fine appearance, a scholar, and an orator.

EUGENIUS (392–394 A.D.).

Eugenius was emperor only in name; while his officer was the power which managed the government. Theodosius marched to the West to avenge the death of Valentinian, and to repress what might have terminated in a persecution of the Christians. Eugenius was taken prisoner and put to death, after a reign of two years (394 A.D.); and Honorius, son of Theodosius, was placed on the throne.

HONORIUS (395–423 A.D.).

Honorius was only six years old when he began to reign; so he was placed under the care of a Vandal named Stilicho, to whom he was allied by marriage. Even in this, the last effort of the Roman empire, the government was made not only respectable, but formidable. The barbarians were driven from the frontiers on the Rhine and in Britain; a revolt in Africa was suppressed; and, having placed the affairs of the West in a state of safety, the emperor went east, and protected Arcadius, who had succeeded Theodosius, from the machinations of his enemies. His chief fame rests on his operations against the more dangerous hordes who were now bursting upon Southern Europe, and whom we shall shortly consider.

Honorius was weak, vacillating, and jealous. The glories of his reign are those of his general, whom he did not scruple to put to death the moment he conceived that his throne could exist without him. The sack of Rome by Alaric followed; and, when this evil was survived, numerous contestants arose in different parts of the empire, each eager for a portion of the fabric which was now so obviously crumbling to pieces. Britain, as usual, took the lead; but the usurper's claims had no stability, and he was quickly supplanted by another. It was not until four rivals, each claiming to be emperor of Rome, had disposed of each other, that Honorius was able to bring the West into subjection. In Gaul and Spain, the same restless spirit was shown.

VALENTINIAN III (423–455 A.D.).

Honorius was succeeded, after one of the longest reigns of the imperial line, by Valentinian III. (423 A.D.). His empire was but a relic of its former self. Gaul, Spain, and Britain were practically lost; Illyria and Pannonia were in the hands of the Goths; and Africa was soon after seized by the barbarians. Valentinian was fortunate in the possession of Ætius, a Scythian by birth, who for a time upheld the Roman name, winning for himself the title of "Last of the Romans." He was assassinated by his ungrateful master.

MAXIMUS (455 A.D.).

A few months later, Valentinian fell by the hand of Maximus, a senator; and the state was relieved of a monster weaker, more cruel, and more contemptible than even Honorius (455 A.D.). The reign of Maximus lasted but three months, and is included in the invasion of the Vandals.

AVITUS (455–456 A.D.).

Maximus was followed by Avitus, a noble of Gaul; but he was deposed the next year by Count Ricimer, and retired to Gaul, where he was soon after assassinated.

RICIMER (457–467 A.D.).

Ricimer was a Sueve, a man of considerable ability. For some time, he managed entirely the affairs of the empire, making and unmaking its monarchs at pleasure. After the removal of Avitus, ten months were allowed to elapse before a successor was appointed; and then the crown was bestowed on a Sueve, named Majoram (457 A.D.). During this reign, an unsuccessful war was waged against the Vandals in Africa, in which the Roman fleet was destroyed off Carthage. This was made an excuse for compelling Majoram to resign. Ricimer now (461 A.D.) placed Libius Severus on the throne, still holding the power in his own hands. Libius was chosen as being too weak and forceless to interfere with the plans of Ricimer. An usurper was finally set up against him, who succeeded in holding Dalmatia for a time unmolested. After the death of Severus, Ricimer ruled under the title of Patrician, when the people demanded an emperor, and he gave them Anthemius, on the recommendation of the emperor of the East.

ANTHEMIUS (467–472 A.D.).

Anthemius attempted to strengthen his position by marrying a daughter of Ricimer; but jealousy soon sprung up between them. Ricimer threw off his allegiance, and invited a horde of barbarians across the Alps, with whom he captured and sacked Rome, and put Anthemius to death. The name of his successor was Olybrius, who died before the end of the year (472 A.D.). In the mean time, Ricimer died of a painful disorder; but his death occurred too late to benefit the doomed empire. Names, which appear only as names, now follow each other so rapidly as to be useless even to mark time as it passed. Glycerus, the successor of Olybrius, was forced to give place to Julius Nepos (474 A.D.), who was compelled to abdicate the following year. Orestes, the leader of the barbarians, who made this change, placed his son on the throne under the name of Augustulus. The barbarians now demanded a third of the land of Italy, which was refused them. Under the lead of Odoacer, they slew Orestes, and deposed his son (476 A.D.). Zeno, emperor of the East, was now persuaded to declare the office of emperor of the West abolished, and to give the government of " the Diocese of Italy " to Odoacer, with the title of " Patrician."

CHAPTER XXXIII.

THE sieges and captures of Rome by the barbarians have been arranged in a chapter by themselves, instead of in their chronological places in the narrative of the emperors, because by this plan a better idea of the operations can be given; and especially because a clearer and more distinct conception of the rise of the nations, which, tearing in pieces the empire of Rome, have made up modern Europe, can be obtained.

The **Huns**, who caused the movement which overturned the western empire, are supposed to have come originally from the eastern portion of Asia, where they were at one time very powerful. A series of defeats gave rise to defection among their tributaries, and soon after (about the time of Trajan) they were overthrown by a tribe of Tartars. A large body of the Huns then went westward, and divided into two branches: one occupied the country east of the Caspian Sea, and became known as the White Huns; while the other turned towards the Volga, and received the name of Black Calmucks of Russia.

The first enemy met by the Huns in Europe were the **Alans**, an Asiatic tribe, which had mingled largely with the Germans. The Alans were brave and warlike, but the march of the Huns was irresistible. The Alans divided into three portions : one escaped to the region between the Black and Caspian Seas; another to Germany, whom we shall again meet; and a third joined the army of the Huns. The defeat of the Alans brought the Huns in contact with the Goths (375 A.D.), a powerful tribe, who lived to the north of the Danube, and who were then ruled by a king named Hermanric.

The Gothic nation consisted of two branches, the Ostrogoths, or eastern Goths, and Visigoths, those living to the west. Hermanric had recently succeeded in uniting these two tribes, and in compelling the kings of the Visigoths to abandon the royal title for that of Judge. He built up a large kingdom for the Ostrogoths; but, on the approach of the Huns, his dependencies fell from him. He and his successor both lost their lives in attempting the defence of their people ; the Ostrogoths were compelled to submit to the Huns, and were absorbed as the Alans had been. A portion, however, escaped southward towards the Roman empire.

The Visigoths, under one of their judges, named Athanaric, at first showed signs of attempting to defend the country between the Pruth and the Danube, but the hideous appearance and wild shouts of the Huns so terrified their young men that they fled back upon the Danube, and besought the Romans to allow them to place the river between them and their enemy. They were allowed to cross, but were compelled to undergo every privation and indignity. The remnant of the Ostrogoths now arrived at the Danube, and they also desired to cross. To them permission was refused ; but fear of the Huns was greater than fear of the Romans. They seized shipping, and crossed the river, despite the prohibition of the empire.

Arrived in the Roman territory, they found their Visigothic brethren in so sad a condition that they united with them to compel from Constantinople the decent treatment refused to their misfortunes. An attempt to assassinate the Gothic judges brought matters to a crisis. The Goths broke into open revolt, and, after defeating the army sent against them, burst into Thrace, ravaging the country as they went. It may be seen that, by their hesitating and perfidious policy, the eastern empire made for itself an enemy, which might easily have been converted into a strong ally against the Huns.

Valens, emperor at Constantinople, sent an army against the Goths, but without obtaining any advantage. He now took the field in person, but was defeated (378 A.D.) and wounded. He was carried to a hut, where he was burned to death. After attempting to capture both Hadrianople and Constantinople, without success, the Goths moved southward and westward into Greece, everywhere ravaging the country.

Many of the Gothic youth had been received as hostages by the Greek (or eastern) empire, and had been scattered through the cities of Asia. These now caused much alarm, lest they should rise to assist their countrymen; so an order was issued for their massacre, and on a certain day they were gathered together, and remorselessly slaughtered. It is well to note the different methods employed by ancient Rome and by her offspring, the Greek empire, in carrying on wars and treating an enemy.

Soon after the massacre of the Gothic youth, the western emperor appointed Theodosius "the Great" to the throne, which had been vacant since the death of Valens. Instead of meeting the barbarians in the field, Theodosius fortified strong points, whence he might watch the enemy, and select a favorable time for an attack. By means of a deserter, he surprised their camp and gained a complete victory. The Goths were now taken into the service of the empire, and the first chapter of the barbarian invasion of the empire was brought to a close. A little later, the Ostrogoths attempted to imitate the exploits of the Visigoths, but were defeated; and the remnant of their army was planted in Lydia and Phrygia.

We now meet two of the great names connected with the fall of Rome, — Alaric and Stilicho. Theodosius was succeeded by Arcadius; and before the end of the year the Goths broke into open revolt, under the leadership of Alaric. Athens was ransomed; Corinth, Argos, and Sparta were taken and plundered. No place was strong enough to offer effectual resistance. At this juncture, Stilicho, general of the western empire, hastened to the scene, and succeeded in surrounding the Goths. Allowing his troops to relax their discipline, Alaric burst through his lines, and escaped. The war was now ended by the Goths making peace with Constantinople; and the pusillanimous court bestowed on Alaric the office of "master-general of Illyrium." How sincere the barbarian was in his offers of peace may be seen from the fact that in two years he invaded Italy (400 A.D.).

The emperor of the West was Honorius, a man so weak that even the genius of Stilicho could not save his name with honor. His most prominent attribute was cowardice; his next, wanton cruelty. No sooner did this ruler of men learn of the approach of Alaric

8

than he hastened to find a place of safety for himself;
while Stilicho should arrange for the defence of the
empire. Troops were called from Britain, Gaul, and
the other provinces far and near, leaving their
places vacant and defenceless. Honorius attempted
to escape to Gaul, but was surprised by the Gothic
cavalry, and took refuge in Asta, a fortified town,
where he was besieged by Alaric until the arrival
of Stilicho, who at once laid siege to the besiegers.
On Easter day, Stilicho attacked the Goths, and utterly
routed them, after a severe and bloody battle. Alaric's
officers were now ready to fall from him; but, good
terms being offered by Stilicho, peace was made. In
his retreat, Alaric attempted to lay siege to Verona;
but he was betrayed, suffered a second defeat fully as
serious as the first, and only escaped by the fleetness
of his horse. It will be seen that in this contest no
faith was kept by any party, Stilicho alone appearing
to possess either manliness or integrity. Honorius
now went to Rome to enjoy the honor of a triumph
· (404 A.D.).

Rome had scarcely time to congratulate herself upon
her escape from the Goths, when a new enemy burst
upon her. Pushing westward, the Huns dislodged the
northern tribes of Germany, dwelling on the Baltic, —
the Alans, Sueves, Vandals, and Burgundians, who
marched south, under the leadership of Radagaisus, to
the number of about two hundred thousand fighting
men. The safety of Italy was again intrusted to Stilicho: the North was abandoned to the invaders.

The troops were speedily recalled, conscription was
rigorously enforced, and every measure was adopted by
which an army could be raised; yet barely thirty or

forty thousand men was the limit of that empire, whose capital alone had placed a much larger force in the field during the days of the republic. To these were added some barbarian auxiliaries, a handful to whom was intrusted the preservation of Rome.

Meeting with no opposition, the army of Radagaisus poured into Italy. They laid siege to Florence, where they were detained by the obstinate bravery of its inhabitants until the arrival of Stilicho. As before, in the case of the Goths, the Romans surrounded the enemy with a fortified camp, and reduced them by hunger. In despair, the barbarians attempted to break through the Roman lines, but were overthrown. Radagaisus surrendered, and was beheaded, after about one-third of his forces had fallen in the battle.

The survivors of the army of Radagaisus burst into Gaul, ravaged the lower portion of the country, and finally separated: one portion, the Burgundians, remained on the frontier, and gave their name to their possessions. There they passed through various vicissitudes, — under their kings, opposing the spread of the Franks; later, under their dukes, peers of the proudest monarchs of Christendom, making alliances or waging war with Germany, France, and England; and finally, after the death of Charles the Bold, passing to the house of Austria, as the inheritance of his daughter, and becoming a bone of contention between France and Germany. The Alans, Sueves, and Vandals pushed into Spain, where they established their kingdoms. The Alans occupied the country at the foot of the Pyrenees, corresponding nearly to modern Catalonia and Aragon. They were soon after subdued by the Visigoths. The Sueves settled in the north-west.

Their territory included modern Galicia, a portion of Leon and Old Castile, and the states bordering on the Bay of Biscay. Like the Alans, they fell a prey to Visigoths, and were absorbed by them. The Vandals occupied the southern portion of Spain, whence they went to Africa, where they maintained themselves for nearly a century, — at one time powerful enough to capture Rome itself, as we shall see, and then being extinguished by the genius of Belisarius.

Rome was now delivered from her enemy; and the emperor no longer needed his general. Stilicho and his friends were attacked by slanderers, who persuaded Honorius that he was plotting for the throne. A wholesale slaughter of his friends ensued; and at length Stilicho himself was put to death at the command of the master whose crown he had twice saved. With Stilicho Rome fell.

Having murdered his general, Honorius ordered a massacre of his foreign troops. Those who escaped naturally looked to Alaric for protection, and to him they went. By this stroke of policy, the empire lost about thirty thousand of its bravest troops. Scarcely two months elapsed after the death of Stilicho before Alaric appeared again in Italy. Pillaging the cities which were in his way, he marched directly on Rome, and, sitting down before it, sought to reduce the city by hunger rather than to capture it by assault. Famine and pestilence raged in the city; and Rome purchased the retreat of her enemy, as she had done that of the Gauls in early times. Alaric was induced to accept the ransom, as an early winter made it necessary for him to provide for his men. He offered peace to the emperor, who, though unable to make resistance, refused to accept it.

The next year, Alaric appeared before Rome a second time, and endeavored to enforce his demands on Honorius by raising Attalus to the throne. Attalus did not show the ability required to maintain his position, and was beset with every trouble. Heraclius, prefect of Africa, stopped the exportation of grain to Italy, — an order which inflicted on Rome the evils of famine. The people rose. Attalus was now deposed by Alaric; and his purple was sent to Honorius as a pledge of peace. The emperor was inexorable; and Alaric marched on Rome a third time. The gates were opened from within; and Rome, after the lapse of eight centuries, became a second time a prey to barbarians (A.D. 410, August 24).

After plundering the city for five days, the Goths marched out of Rome, and ravaged the country. But the days of Alaric were almost spent. Before the end of the year, he died, after a brief illness; and, a little later, Rome saw his army, under the leadership of his brother-in-law, march into France, there to establish a kingdom which should reach from the Loire and the Rhone to the Straits of Gibraltar. They were gradually overcome in France, and their possessions restricted to Spain. They were overwhelmed by the Arabs in their invasion of Spain, but escaped to the mountains, and there, preserving their religion and their race, handed them down to their descendants, the modern Spaniards.

The Germans had been a source of constant annoyance to the Romans. Defeat only compelled them to return to their impregnable forests, whence they would issue on the first opportunity. When Stilicho first assumed the duties of master-general of the armies, he made a rapid journey down the Rhine for the purpose of converting these troublesome enemies into friends, on whom he could rely for the defence of the boundaries of Gaul. In this he succeeded so well that, when the remains of the army of Radagaisus invaded the country, they were met by a determined resistance, which nearly proved fatal to the Vandalic portion of the army. From this time, they lived in firm friendship with Rome, maintaining the strictest fidelity to the empire until her fall.

At length, prompted by the example of the Burgundians and Visigoths, they began a series of attempts to enlarge their boundaries, under their king, Clodion, who, in a reign of twenty-five years, established himself firmly in all the country from the Rhine to the Somme. He attempted to surprise lower Belgium, but was defeated by Ætius, of whom we shall see more, and was compelled to retreat. Clodion returned soon after (447 A.D.) ; and the Franks thenceforth possessed the land, giving their name to the country, and establishing the present French nation in France. The death of Clodion left two pretenders to his throne; and, although by German custom the sons of the deceased monarch should have divided his possessions between them, both of these worthies sought to obtain the whole kingdom. The elder appealed to the Huns to support him in his pretensions; the younger, Merovius, looked to Rome for aid.

The narrative now returns to the Huns. Instead of uniting for the settlement of some portion of Russia or northern Germany, the Huns confined their operations to predatory excursions, scarcely recognizing any authority but their own individual wills. Their chief seat was the country now known as Hungary, from a fancied connection with them of the Magyars, who occupied it in the ninth century. The Huns were now ruled by two kings named Attila and Bleda; but Bleda was speedily murdered by his brother; and Attila, " the Scourge of God," ruled alone over their wild hordes. The portrait of Attila is thus painted. His features bore the mark of his eastern origin. He had a large head, a swarthy complexion, small, deep-seated eyes, a flat nose, a few hairs in place of a beard, broad shoulders, and a short, square body of nervous strength, though disproportioned form. This man wielded at will an army of, legends say, five, or even seven, hundred thousand men ; a statement to be received with a liberal allowance for exaggeration.

The first operations of Attila were against the eastern empire, whose armies he overthrew in the field, and he afterward even appeared before the walls of Constantinople (441. A.D.). It was to the Huns that the Vandals owed much of their success in Africa; for the empire was obliged to recall in haste, for its own protection, the soldiers who had been intended for the chastising of that bold band of barbarians. The advent of Marcian to the eastern throne ended the sufferings of that empire at the hands of the Huns. By his peaceful yet firm demeanor, he so impressed Attila that he allowed his attentions to be diverted towards the West.

It was at this time that Attila received the invitation of the son of Clodion to interfere in the affairs of Gaul. He was then threatening both empires with invasion ; but the prospect of an ally in Gaul, with an opportunity of afterwards attacking Italy from the

West, was too favorable to be neglected. The Romans were perfectly willing to transfer the scene of conflict from Italy to Gaul, where they might expect a valuable ally in Theodoric, king of the Visigoths. The Stilicho of this contest was Ætius, " the Last of the Romans," who had already won the confidence of his master by his bold operations in Gaul; and the respect of his adversary, to whom he was personally known, by an exhibition of such virtues as were most likely to win the esteem of a savage.

A march of six hundred miles brought the Huns to the Rhine, which they crossed in the winter; and, continuing their progress, they sacked and burned the cities they found on their way. Metz fell; but Troyes was saved by the courage of its bishop, St. Loup, and Orleans by that of Agnanus, supplemented by the bravery and courage of its citizens and soldiers.

After some delay, the Visigoths decided to take part with the Romans; and both armies appeared before Orleans, after the Huns were within the city, but in time to save it from plunder. Attila now began a cautious retreat, followed so closely by the allies that the Huns lost fifteen thousand men before they arrived at Chalons, where the great battle was fought, which saved, perhaps, the civilization of western Europe from a fate as severe as befell that of Russia, at the hands of the Tartars, some centuries later. Attila began the attack, though warned of his defeat by his soothsayers. He was bravely met by the Romans; and a charge of the Visigoths, who had lost their king in the fight, under his son, the Voan Torresiend, completed the discomfiture of the savages. Night alone saved the hosts of Attila from utter destruction (451 A.D.).

Ætius refused to push the Huns to extremities, and permitted them to retreat, which they did in the direction of Italy, being followed by the prudent Merovius, who each night lighted up the neighboring hills with watch-fires, until his enemy was well past the furthest limits of his possessions. It was this Merovius who gave name to the first dynasty of French monarchs, the Merovingians.

For some indiscretion, Honoria, princess of the western empire, had been banished to Constantinople. While there, she sent to Attila, offering herself as his bride, and urging him to demand her as already betrothed to him. At first, Attila had paid no attention to her message; but the advantage of having a claim on Italy induced him to demand her hand of the emperor. The affairs in Gaul prevented immediate action on his receiving a refusal; but, now these were decided, he marched on Italy, to enforce his demand and grow rich with plunder. For three weeks, Aquileia resisted his efforts (for, as we must have noticed, the barbarians were seldom successful in the siege of a bravely defended walled city); but an unguarded portion of the wall was finally discovered, and Aquileia was swept from the face of the earth. The " Scourge " raged over the whole country, only sparing those who preserved their lives by the surrender of their wealth.

It was to this invasion that Venice owed its rise. The inhabitants who fled from the approach of the Huns found on the islands in the lagoons, at the head of the Adriatic, a harbor of safety. There they planted the seeds of the republic whose ships so long carried the commerce of the world, who maintained her liberties till within a century, and now at length, within a

8*   L

few years, has been reunited with Italy under one government, with Rome as its capital.

Rome now sent an embassy to Attila, among whom was Leo the Great, who, by the promise of the hand of Honoria, purchased peace. Attila died soon after from the bursting of a blood-vessel (453 A.D.), and at his death the empire of the Huns ceased to exist. Honoria was punished for her share in the misfortunes of her country by marriage with an obscure husband, and was then condemned to perpetual imprisonment.

The story of Stilicho is the story of Ætius. When the empire was safe, and the general was no longer necessary, he was murdered, — stabbed by the emperor with his own hands. By the wanton insult of one of his subjects, named Maximus (455 A.D., March 16), Valentinian lost his life. Maximus seized the throne, and forcibly married the empress Eudoxia. As if still further to insure her enmity, he confessed to her the murder of her husband, and she determined to rid herself of her master at any cost. She could expect no aid from the East; so she turned to Genseric, king of the Vandals, who had established themselves in Africa, making Carthage their capital, and were ravaging the coasts of the Mediterranean with a large fleet.

Genseric was in Sicily when the message arrived, and at once set sail for the mouth of the Tiber. Maximus attempted to escape, but was killed with stones by the populace (June 12). The evil had been done. Genseric left Ostia three days later; the city was delivered into his hands on promise of sparing the property of the church, and for fourteen days the barbarians ravaged it at pleasure. Among the spoils taken were the sacred implements of the temple, which

Titus had brought from Jerusalem ; but the vessel which carried them was lost at sea or in the Tiber. Genseric left Rome, which he could not hope to hold, taking with him Eudoxia, the author of the disaster, and her daughters, one of whom he married to his son.

The rest has been told : it is only the story of the misrule of Count Ricimer, and the final abolishing of the western empire. Of the twenty-one years between the capture of the city by Genseric and the end of the empire, all but three belong to the rule of Ricimer ; and the condition in which he left his charge may be judged from its sudden death, only three years after he had made himself master of its capital by force.

Rome soon after began to regain her power by means of the Church, of which she became the chief seat ; and soon we find her exercising an absolute sway over the monarchs of Europe, deposing them when obdurate, and rewarding them when obedient. A little more than three hundred years after the fall of the western empire, it was revived by the coronation of Charlemagne, king of France, at Rome ; and an attempt was made to transmit the title of emperor to his posterity. Charlemagne had added Germany to the kingdom of the Franks, and had done much to Christianize and civilize the country. It was soon, however, sundered from France ; and the imperial title passed over to Germany, whose monarch claimed to be the head of the Holy Roman Empire. The first Napoleon is said also to have had a desire to restore the western empire, with France as its corner-stone, but did not accomplish it. The western empire is now dead, and in its place we have the kingdom of Italy, with Rome as its capital.

The eastern empire dragged on a miserable existence, until about thirty-eight years before the discovery of America by Columbus, when it was overthrown by the Turks, an Asiatic people, who, like the Huns, owed their march into the West to the victories of the Tartars. The dissensions of the eastern empire were but the partial cause of its downfall. It was utterly demoralized. The Arabs had taken from it all of Asia, the North had fallen away, Constantinople had been captured by the French. It fell because it was ripe, — over-ripe, rotten to the core ; and the Turkish empire by which it was succeeded is now fast fading away.

CHAPTER XXXIV.

ROMAN LITERATURE.*

PLAUTUS (254–184 B.C.).

ONE of the earliest Roman writers was **Plautus**, the comic poet. He was born at **Sarsina**, in Umbria, of free but poor parents. He at first worked on the stage at Rome, but lost his savings through speculation. He then for some time worked in a treadmill, and afterwards gained his subsistence by Latin versions of Greek comedies, until his death.

Twenty of his plays are extant.

ENNIUS (139–69 B.C.).

Quintus Ennius gained great renown as an **epic** poet. He was born at **Rudiæ**, served in the Roman army in Sardinia, and was taken to Rome by Marcus Porcius Cato. Here he gained a livelihood by giving instruction in Greek. His first poem, the "**Annales**," relates the traditional Roman history, from Æneas's arrival in Italy down to the poet's own day.

TERENCE (195–159 B.C.).

Publius Terentius (Afer), the **comic** poet, was a native of Carthage, but at an early age came to Rome, where he was the slave of a senator, Terentius, by

---

* Taken mostly from Teuffel's " Roman Literature."

whom he was educated like a freeman and soon liberated.   He wrote six comedies, all of which are
preserved.

CICERO (106–43 B.C.).

Marcus Tullius Cicero was born January 6, 106 B.C.,
at Arpinum. He was the son of a Roman knight. He
employed every means of studying rhetoric in all
its branches, and pleaded his first cause under Sulla's
dictatorship.   To perfect himself still further, he spent
two years (79–77 B.C.) in Greece and Asia.   He was
afterwards Quæstor in Sicily (75 B.C.), Ædilis curulis
(72 B.C.), Prætor urbanus (66 B.C.), and Consul (63 B.C.).
The Catilinarian conspiracy, which broke out during
Cicero's consulship, was suppressed by him.   In 58 B.C.,
Cicero was exiled by the first triumvirate.   During his
exile, he lived in Thessalonica and Dyrrachium.   One
year later, he was allowed to return to Rome.   From
July 51 to July 52 B.C., he was proconsul over the
province Cilicia.

On his return to Rome, the contention between
Cæsar and the Senate, with Pompey at its head, had
already broken out. After some hesitation, Cicero joined
Pompey at Dyrrachium, with whom he remained until
the battle of Pharsalus, 48 B.C.   The next year Cicero
lived at Brundisium, awaiting permission from Cæsar
to return to Rome.   The next two years were spent in
literary occupations.   His Philippics, delivered against
Antony, caused his proscription by the second triumvirate, and subsequent murder, December, 743 B.C.

Cicero was endowed by nature with great talents.
But he was always under the sway of the moment,

and therefore little qualified to be a statesman; yet he had not sufficient self-knowledge to see it. Hence the attempts he made to play a part in politics served only to lay bare his utter weakness. Thus it happened that he was used and then pushed aside, attracted and repelled, deceived by the weakness of his friends and the strength of his adversaries; and at last threatened by both extreme parties, between which he tried to steer his way.

As an orator, Cicero had a very happy natural talent. The extreme versatility of his mind; his lively imagination; his great sensitiveness; his inexhaustible richness of expression, which was never at a loss for a word or tone to suit any circumstance or mood; his felicitous memory; his splendid voice and impressive figure, — all contributed to render him an excellent orator.

But he himself did every thing to attain perfection. Not until he had spent a long time in laborious study and preparation did he make his *début* as an orator; nor did he ever rest and think himself perfect, but was always working, and never pleaded a cause without careful preparation. Each success was to him only a step to another still higher achievement; and by continual meditation and study he kept himself fully prepared for his task. Hence he succeeded, as is now universally admitted, in gaining a place beside Demosthenes, or at all events immediately after him.

There are extant **fifty-seven** orations of Cicero, and fragments of **twenty** more.

In **rhetoric**, Cicero was a disciple of the Greeks. His chief writings on this subject are as follows : —

De Inventione (an early and unripe production).

De Oratore, three books.

Brutus, De Claris Oratoribus.

Orator ad M. Brutum.

The correspondence of Cicero was great, and furnishes an inexhaustible treasure of contemporaneous history. There are extant eight hundred and sixty-four letters upon both personal and political matters.

Cicero was a lover of **philosophy**. His writings on this subject are as follows : —

De Republica.

De Legibus.

De Finibus Bonorum et Malorum.

Academica.

Tusculanæ Disputationes.

De Natura Deorum.

De Senectute, or Cato Major.

De Divinatione.

De Amicitia, or Laelius.

De Officiis.

CÆSAR (100–44 B.C.).

Caius Julius Cæsar was born July 12, 100 B.C. As he was related to Marius, his life was in danger when Sulla was victorious. He served in Asia in 80 B.C., and commenced his oratorical and political career with charges of extortion against members of the nobility. He then continued his studies in Rhodes (79 B.C.), became Quæstor (67 B.C.) in Hispania ulterior, Ædile (65 B.C.), Pontifex maximus (63 B.C.), Prætor (62 B.C.), Proprætor in Hispania ulterior (61 B.C.), Consul (59 B.C.). He was proconsul in Gaul (58–50 B.C.), which he subjugated and rearranged; but at the same time he opened numerous resources to himself, and trained an army. By means of this, he gained absolute power in the years 49–46 B.C. He was murdered the 15th of March, 44 B.C.

Cæsar possessed the most varied talents. Hardly an orator of his times spoke Latin so well. Of his literary works, the most important are the **"Commentarii,"** containing the history of the first seven years of the **Gallic** war, in **seven** books; and the history of the **Civil** war, down to the **Alexandrine** war, in **three** books.

After Cæsar's death, his nearest friends thought it incumbent upon them to describe also those expeditions which he had not narrated himself ; viz., his last year in Gaul, and the Alexandrine, African, and Spanish wars. They are by **three** writers. **Aulus Hirtius** probably wrote the account of his last year in Gaul and the Alexandrine war.

Nepos (94–24 B.C.).

Cornelius Nepos was born in Upper Italy, and was a friend of both Cicero and Atticus. He was a prolific writer; but only a portion of one of his works, " De Viris Illustribus," has come down to us, which shows neither historical accuracy nor good style.

Lucretius (98–55 B.C.).

Titus Lucretius Carus has left a didactic poem, "**De Rerum Natura,**" in six books. The tone pervading the work is sad, and in many places even bitter.

Sallust (87–34 B.C.).

Caius Sallustius Crispus, of Amiternum, has left two **historical** productions : " **Catilina,**" or **Conspiracy of**

Catiline ; and " Jugurtha," or the Jugurthine War. His style is rhetorical, and often chronologically inaccurate. Sallust excels in delineations of character. He took great pains in his composition ; and, following Thucydides as a model, he endeavored to be brief and concise, even so as to become oftentimes obscure.

CATULLUS (87–47 B.C.).

Caius Valerius Catullus, of Verona, is the greatest lyric poet of Roman literature. One hundred and sixteen of his poems are preserved.

VERGIL (70–19 B.C.).

Publius Vergilius Maro was born at Andes, near Mantua, October 15, 70 B.C. He was educated at Cremona and Mediolanum. After completing his education, he retired to his paternal estate. In the division of land among the soldiers after the battle of Philippi (42 B.C.), Vergil was deprived of his property; but it was afterwards restored, at the command of Octavius. After this, Vergil lived partly at Rome, partly in Campania. His health was poor. He died at Brundisium in his fifty-second year, September 22, 19 B.C.

Vergil was of a childlike, innocent, and amiable disposition, a good son and faithful friend, honest, and full of devotion to persons and ideal interests, but not competent to grapple with the tasks and difficulties of practical life.

His extant poems are as follows : —

1. Bucolica, ten eclogues, written in 44–42 B.C., and imitated and partially translated from Theocritus.

2. Georgica, in four books, written in 37–30 B.C.

The first book treats of agriculture; the second, of the cultivation of trees; the third, of domestic animals; and the fourth, of bees. The poem is considered the most perfect production of Roman art-poetry.

3. Æneis, in twelve books, commenced 29 B.C., and not finished when the poet died, and published contrary to his express wish. The Æneid gives an account of the wanderings of Æneas from Troy to Italy, and his struggles in Italy to found a city for his followers, from whom descended the Romans.

HORACE (65–8 B.C.).

Quintus Horatius Flaccus, the poet, was born at Venusia, but received his education at Rome and Athens. Of his poems, we have four books of Odes, one of his Epodes, two books of Satires, two books of Epistles, and the Ars Poetica.

TIBULLUS (54–29 B.C.).

Albius Tibullus, an elegiac poet, celebrated in exquisitely fine poems the beauty and cruelty of his mistresses.

PROPERTIUS (49–15 B.C.).

Sextus Propertius was a native of Umbria, but educated at Rome. He also is an elegiac poet, and treats mostly of love.

OVID (43 B.C.–18 A.D.).

Publius Ovidius Naso, a native of Sulmo, devoted himself exclusively to poetry, for which he had uncommon talent. His writings consist of three books of Amores; one of the Heroides; the Ars Amatoria; Remedia Amoris; the Metamorphoses (fifteen books); the Tristia; the Fasti.

LIVY (59 B.C. – 17 A.D.).

Titus Livius, the most important prose writer of the Augustine period, was a native of Patavium (Padua), a man of rhetorical training, and who spent the greater part of his life at Rome. His history of Rome, from the foundation of the city until the death of Drusus, consisted of one hundred and forty-two books, of which only thirty-five have come down to us.

PHÆDRUS.

Phædrus, a writer of fables, flourished in the reign of Tiberius (14–37 A.D.). He was originally a slave, brought from Thrace or Macedonia. His fables are ninety-seven in number, and written in Iambic verse.

SENECA (4 B.C. – 64 A.D.).

Lucius Annæus Seneca, among other things, wrote tragedies, eight in number. He was born at Corduba, in Spain.

CURTIUS.

Quintus Curtius Rufus wrote, during the reign of Claudius (41–54 A.D.), the Historiæ de Rebus Gestis Alexandri Magni, in ten books.

PERSIUS (34–62 A.D.).

Among the poets of the time of Nero, the youthful Aulus Persius Flaccus, of Volaterræ, wrote six satires, which are of an obscure style, and hard to understand.

Lucan (39–65 A.D.).

Marcus Annæus Lucanus, nephew of Seneca, was a fertile writer in both prose and poetry. We possess his Pharsalia, in ten books, an unfinished epic poem on the civil war between Cæsar and Pompey.

Pliny the Elder (23–79 A.D.).

Caius Plinius Secundus, of Upper Italy, was a great scholar in history, grammar, rhetoric, and natural science. Of his writings, we possess one on Natural History, in thirty-seven books.

Statius (45–96 A.D.).

Publius Papinius Statius, of Naples, had considerable poetical genius. His largest work is the Thebaid. He also wrote the Achilleis (unfinished) and the Silvæ.

Martial (42–102 A.D.).

Marcus Valerius Martialis, from Bilbilis, in Spain, wrote epigrams, of which we have fifteen books.

Quintilian (35–95 A.D.).

Marcus Fabius Quintilianus, of Calagurris, in Spain, was educated at Rome, and a public professor of eloquence in that city. He wrote a volume, in twelve books, on the complete training of an orator, — "De Institutione Oratoria."

JUVENAL (47–130 A.D.).

Decimus Junius Juvenalis, of Aquinum, was a great satirist. We have sixteen of his Satires, describing the vices of Roman society in an eloquent manner.

TACITUS (54–119 A.D.).

Cornelius Tacitus was the great historian of this period. His birthplace is unknown. His works are as follows: —

1. **Dialogus de Oratoribus.**
2. **De Vita et Moribus Julii Agricolæ Liber,** a biography of Tacitus's father-in-law.
3. **De Moribus et Populis Germaniæ,** an ethnographical description of the Germans.
4. **Historiæ,** a narrative of the events of the reigns of Galba, Otho, Vespasian, Titus, and Domitian.
5. **Annales,** a history of the reign of **Tiberius, Caligula, Claudius,** and **Nero.**

PLINY THE YOUNGER (62–113 A.D.).

Caius Plinius Cæcilius Secundus, the adopted son of Pliny the Elder, of Comum, composed letters, of which we have nine books. These letters touch a large number of subjects, and their diction is fluent and smooth.

CHAPTER XXXV.

Viæ Romanæ.*

Via = a public road. It was not until the time of the Samnite wars that the Romans felt the necessity of securing a safe means of communication between the city and their armies.

The first great public road was the **Via Appia,** which extended at first from Rome to Capua, and was made in 312 B.C.

The general construction of the Roman road was as follows : In the first place, two shallow trenches (sulci) were dug parallel to each other, marking the breadth of the proposed road, which was from thirteen to fifteen feet. The loose earth between the trenches was then removed, and the excavation continued until a solid foundation (gremium) was reached, upon which the materials of the road might firmly rest. If this could not be attained in consequence of the swampy nature of the ground, or from any peculiarity in the soil, a basis was formed artificially by driving piles (festucationes). Above the **gremium** were **four** distinct strata. The lowest was the **statumen,** consisting of stones not smaller than the hand could just grasp ; above the statumen was the **rudus,** a mass of broken stones cemented with lime, rammed down hard, and **nine** inches thick.

* From Dr. Smith's Dictionary of Antiquities.

Above the rudus came the **nucleus**, composed of fragments of brick and pottery, the pieces being smaller
than in the rudus, cemented with lime, and **six** inches
thick. Uppermost was the **pavimentum**, composed
of large polygonal blocks of the hardest stone (silex),
irregular in form, but fitted and jointed with the
greatest nicety, so as to present a perfectly even
surface.

Regular foot-paths were raised upon each side, and
strewed with gravel.

Stone blocks were set up at moderate intervals on
the side of the foot-paths, in order that travellers on
horseback might be able to mount without assistance.
Finally, **milestones** were erected along the whole extent of the great highways, marking the distances from
Rome.

The chief roads which issued from Rome were:—

1. **Via Appia**, passing through **Capua, Beneventum,
Tarentum**, and ending at **Brundisium**.

2. **Via Latina**, passing through **Aquinum, Teanum**,
and joining the Via Appia at **Beneventum**.

3. **Via Flaminia**, the great north road. It proceeded
nearly north of **Ocriculum** and **Narnia**, in Umbria.
Here a branch struck off, making a sweep to the east
through **Spoletium**, and joined the main trunk at **Ful-
ginia**. It continued through **Fanum, Flaminii**, and
Nuceria, where it again divided, one line running
nearly straight to **Fanum Fortunæ**, on the Adriatic;
while the other, diverging to **Ancona**, continued from
there along the coast to **Fanum Fortunæ**, where the two
branches, uniting, passed on to **Ariminum** through **Pi-
saurum**. From here, it was extended, under the name of
Via Æmilia, and traversed the heart of Cisalpine Gaul

through Bononia, Mutina, Parma, Placentia (where it crossed the Po), to Mediolanum.

4. Via Aurelia, the great coast road, reached the coast at Alsium, and followed the shore along Etruria and Liguria, by Genoa, as far as Forum Julii, in Gaul.

There were numerous other smaller roads.

9   M

CHAPTER XXXVI.

PROVINCIÆ.*

Provincia (shortened form of providentia). After Italy had been conquered by Rome, all the countries added to the Roman dominions were called **Provinciæ**. Sicily was the first country made a province. A conquered country either received its provincial organization from the Roman commander, whose acts required the approval of the Senate; or the government was organized by the commander, and a body of commissioners were appointed by the Senate out of their own number. The mode of dealing with a conquered country was not uniform. When constituted a province, it did not become to all purposes an integral part of the Roman state: it retained its national existence, though it lost its sovereignty. At first, **prætors** were appointed to govern the provinces; but afterwards persons who had been prætors were appointed, at the expiration of their office, with the title of **Proprætor**. In later times of the republic, the consuls also, after the expiration of their year of office, received the government of a province, with the title of **Proconsuls**: such provinces were called **Provinciæ Consulares**. The provinces were generally distributed by lot; but their distribution

* From Dr. Smith's Dictionary of Antiquities.

was sometimes arranged by agreement among the persons entitled to them. A province was generally held for a year; but the time was often prolonged. When a new governor arrived in his province, his predecessor was required to leave it within thirty days.

The governor was assisted by two **quæstors,** who received from the Roman treasury the necessary sums for the administration of the province, and who also collected most of the taxes.

The Roman provinces, up to the battle of Actium, were as follows: —

1. Sicilia.
2. Sardinia and Corsica.
3. Hispania Citerior.
4. Hispania Ulterior.
5. Gallia Citerior.
6. Gallia Narbonensis.
7. Illyricum.
8. Macedonia.
9. Achaia.
10. Asia.
11. Cilicia.
12. Syria.
13. Bithynia and Pontus. ·
14. Cyprus.
15. Africa.
16. Cyrenaica and Creta.
17. Numidia.
18. Mauritania.

CHAPTER XXXVII.

LEGENDARY ROME.

Æneas, son of Anchises and Venus, fled from Troja, after its capture by the Greeks (1184 B.C.), and came to Italy with his son and a number of followers. Latinus, who was king of the region where Æneas landed, received him kindly and gave him his daughter Lavinia in marriage. Æneas then founded a city and named it Lavinium, in honor of his wife. After the death of Æneas, his son Ascanius became king. He transferred the capital to another place, and founded a new city on Mount Albanus, which he called Alba Longa. A number of kings ruled in succession at Alba Longa, until Silvius Procas, who left two sons, Numitor and Amulius. Amulius, who was the younger, gave his brother the choice of the throne or his father's property. Numitor chose the property; and thus Amulius became king.

Numitor had two children, a son and daughter. Amulius, fearing that they might aspire to the throne, had the son murdered, and made the daughter, named Rhea Silvia, a vestal virgin. These vestal virgins were not permitted to marry. She, however, became pregnant by Mars, and brought forth twin-sons, whom she called Romulus and Remus. When Amulius discovered this, he cast Rhea into prison, and ordered the boys to be thrown into the Tiber.

At this time, the Tiber had overflown its banks; and, since the boys had been placed in a shallow place, the water, when it subsided, left them on dry land. A she-wolf, hearing their cries, ran to them and suckled them. **Faustulus,** a shepherd of this neighborhood, seeing this, took up the boys and carried them home.

Romulus and Remus, thus saved, when they grew up and found out who their mother had been, killed Amulius and restored the kingdom to their grandfather Numitor. Then (753 B.C.) they founded a city upon Mount Aventinus, which Romulus called **Rome** from his own name. While they were surrounding this city with walls, Remus was **killed** in a quarrel with his brother.

Romulus, first king of Rome (753–716 B.C.). Romulus found that he needed citizens to people the city; so, to increase the number of citizens, he opened an asylum, to which many refugees fled. But wives were wanting. To supply this want, Romulus celebrated games, and invited the neighboring people to join in the celebration. When they were all busily engaged in looking on, the Romans suddenly rushed in and snatched away the virgins who were present. This bold robbery caused a war with the Sabines (the people from whom the virgins were stolen), which finally ended in a compromise, and a sharing of the city with the Sabines.

Romulus then chose a hundred senators, and called them **Patres.** He divided the people into thirty wards. He died in the thirty-seventh year of his reign.

Numa Pompilius (716–673 B.C.). After the death of Romulus, there was an interreign of one year. Then **Numa Pompilius,** of **Cures,** a city in the Sabine territory, was appointed king. He was a great law-giver, and also instituted many sacred rites for the purpose of civilizing his uncultivated subjects. He died in the forty-third year of his reign.

Tullus Hostilius (673–641 B.C.). His reign was noted for the destruction of **Alba Longa.**

Ancus Marcius (640–616 B.C.). Ancus was the grandson of Numa, and was like his grandfather in character. He conquered the Latins, enlarged the city, and built new walls around it. He was the first to build a prison. He also founded a city at the mouth of the Tiber, which he called **Ostia.**

Lucius Tarquinius Priscus (616–578 B.C.). Tarquin was a native of Corinth, and had fled into Etruria; from there he went to Rome. At Rome, he became a favorite of king Ancus, and was appointed by him guardian of his children. Tarquin took the government from the sons. He increased the senators whom Romulus appointed by one hundred. He also carried on with success a great many wars, and increased considerably the territory of the city. He introduced a system of drainage, and began the capital. He was killed in the thirty-eighth year of his reign by the sons of Ancus, from whom he had snatched the kingdom.

Servius Tullius (578–534 B.C.). Servius was the son of a female slave, and the son-in-law of king Tarquin. He enlarged the city, and took a census of all. It was found that the city and suburbs contained eighty-three thousand souls. Servius was killed by his daughter **Tullia** and her husband Tarquinius Superbus, the son of Tarquinius Priscus.

Lucius Tarquinius Superbus (534–510 B.C.) was energetic in war, and conquered many neighboring peoples.

He built a temple in honor of Jupiter on the Capitoline Hill. Soon after, Tarquin laid siege to Ardea, a city of the Rutulians, and captured it.

Lucius Brutus Collatinus, and several others, now conspired against the king, who had violated Lucretia, the wife of Collatinus. They closed the gates of the city against him. Tarquin fled with his wife and children.

A republic was then established, and **two consuls** ruled instead of one king. Tarquin made **three** attempts to recover the power at Rome, all unsuccessful. In the last attempt (508 B.C.), Porsena, king of the Etruscans, assisted Tarquin. The contest was decided by the battle of Lake **Regillus.** Tarquin fled to Cumae, and there died.

Coriolanus was one of the heroes of Roman legendary history ; also **Cincinnatus,** for accounts of whom, see Classical Dictionary.

CHRONOLOGY.

(The dates up to 389 B.C. are conjectural.)

B.C.

753.	Foundation of Rome.
753–716.	Reign of Romulus.
716–673.	Reign of Numa Pompilius.
673–641.	Reign of Tullus Hostilius.
640–616.	Reign of Ancus Marcius.
616–578.	Reign of Tarquinius Priscus.
578–534.	Reign of Servius Tullius.
534–510.	Reign of Tarquinius Superbus.
509.	Establishment of the Republic.
494.	Tribuni Plebis.
451.	The Decemviri.
389.	Capture of Rome by the Gauls.
366.	{ Laws of **Licinius** and **Sextius**, aiming to make the Patricians and Plebeians equal at Rome.
343–341.	First Samnite War.
340–338.	The Latin War.
326–304.	Second Samnite War.
298–290.	Third Samnite War.
290.	Romans the Chief People in Italy.
274.	Defeat of Pyrrhus.
264–241.	First Punic War.
219–202.	Second Punic War.
260.	Victory off Mylæ by Duilius.
241.	Victory off Ægates Insulæ.
218.	**Ticinus, Trebia.**
217.	**Trasimenus.**
216.	**Cannæ.**

B.C.

207.	**Metaurus.**
202.	**Zama.**
200–160.	The Romans conquer the East.
150.	The Romans conquer Spain.
146.	Destruction of Carthage.
133.	Tiberius Gracchus.
123–121.	Caius Gracchus.
111–106.	Jugurthine War.
102.	The Cimbri and Teutones.
91–89.	The Italian War.
88–82.	Sulla and Marius quarrel.
74–61.	{ Cnæus Pompeius victorious over Rome's Rebels.
58–49.	Julius Cæsar in Gaul.
49–48.	War between Cæsar and Pompey.
48.	**Pharsalus.**
44.	Murder of Cæsar.
42.	**Philippi.**
31.	**Actium.**

THE EMPIRE.

A.D.

30–14.	Reign of Augustus.
14–37.	Reign of Tiberius.
37–41.	Reign of Caligula.
41–54.	Reign of Claudius.
54–68.	Reign of Nero.
68.	End of **Julian** Emperors.
69.	Beginning of **Flavian** Emperors.
69–79.	Reign of Vespasian.
70.	Destruction of Jerusalem.
79–81.	Reign of Titus.

9*

A.D.

81–96.	Reign of Domitian.
98–117.	Reign of Trajan.
117–138.	Reign of Hadrian.
138–161.	Reign of Antoninus Pius.
161–180.	Reign of Aurelius Antoninus.
180–192.	Reign of Commodus Antoninus.
192–284.	From Pertinax to Diocletian.
284–337.	From Diocletian to Constantine's death.
337–476.	From Constantine to Romulus Augustulus.

INDEX.

[The numbers refer to the pages.]

Cambridge: Press of John Wilson & Son.

www.ingramcontent.com/pod-product-compliance
Lightning Source LLC
Chambersburg PA
CBHW020615030726
47497CB00007B/2259